Renee was taking a risk.
A very big risk.

But it would be worth it, she thought. It had to be.

Meeting Chris Foster again was harder than she thought it would be. He looked nothing like her late husband, Marc, for which she was grateful. She didn't know if she could go through with her plan if he'd even remotely resembled his brother.

She could do this, she thought. She *would* do this. She lifted her head and met his steady gaze. His eyes were the color of pale amber, framed by long black lashes. They reminded her of a panther she'd seen on a television documentary. The cat had been a dangerous and deadly predator. She hoped Chris Foster didn't share those traits.

"I will agree to the terms of your latest offer. If..." She paused and swallowed. Her mouth felt dry. "If," she continued, "you will find something Marc took from my family." *Please, God,* she prayed. *Please let him accept my offer....*

CARLA FREDD

Birmingham, Alabama, native Carla Fredd began her writing career in 1992. After several failed attempts to complete her first book, Ms. Fredd used her skills as an electrical engineer to solve the problem—she got help. She took several creative writing classes, joined Georgia Romance Writers and Romance Writers of America. Her first book, *Fire and Ice,* was released in October 1995 and appeared on the Brentano's Top 20 Bestselling Mass Market list. Her other works include "Matchmaker" one of three stories in Arabesque's *A Valentine Kiss* anthology, and *If Only You Knew.*

Ms. Fredd resides in Georgia and is currently working on her next project.

CARLA FREDD

THE PERFECT MAN

KIMANI™
ROMANCE

KIMANI PRESS™

ISBN-13: 978-0-373-86068-5

THE PERFECT MAN

Printed in U.S.A.

Kimani Romance proudly presents

Every marriage has a secret—or three...

Don't miss this exciting, three-book series
featuring three of the best-loved romance authors

This Time for Good by Carmen Green
available May 2008

The Perfect Man by Carla Fredd
available June 2008

Just Deserts by Brenda Jackson
available July 2008

*Alexandria, Renee and Danielle are three very different
women with one thing in common: their late husband!*

Chapter 1

May

Fear clamped around her throat, leaving a cold, metallic taste in her mouth. Renee Mitchell Foster dropped the pen and stared at the initials on the check-in form for her great-aunt's safe-deposit box. All but the last set of initials were hers. The last entry was made at the end of March and the initials belonged to her husband, Marc, who'd died last month.

Marc had no legitimate reason to have access to Aunt Gert's safe-deposit box.

The cool air from the air-conditioning vents and

her crisp linen pantsuit couldn't touch the hot wave of fear that had her trembling in the vault of the National Bank of Alabama.

She tried to take a deep, calming breath like she'd learned from years of yoga class. A technique she'd used many times in the past.

Marc couldn't have gotten access to the box, she thought, trying to alleviate her fears with cold, hard reason when deep-breathing exercises didn't work.

Her hands shook as she set the card on a table. Slowly she reached inside her purse and took out her Palm. With a few taps of her stylus, she opened the file that listed all the items inside the safe-deposit box and set the organizer on the table.

She lifted the hinged top and looked inside. The thin, black velvet jewelry case, which usually sat on top of all the saving bonds, insurance papers and the deed to her great-aunt's house, was gone. She could feel the blood drain from her face.

"Oh, God, Marc. How could you take it?"

Renee closed her eyes and leaned her shoulder against the wall of locked boxes to keep from falling. She pressed her cheek against the cold metal. The diamond necklace that her great-aunt treasured and loved was gone. The necklace that she'd placed around Renee's neck when she was six and made her feel wanted when her parents had left her in boarding school. The necklace was more than a piece of jewelry. It was the one thing her great-aunt had left from the man she'd loved.

She'd never let anyone wear it except Renee. Now, it was gone.

She pushed against the wall and stood up straight. *Maybe I just overlooked it.* Even as the thought materialized, she didn't believe it in her heart.

She took out every item inside the box, hoping the jewelry case was there under the papers. When she'd pulled out the last item, she realized that her husband had betrayed her yet again. Everything was accounted for except the diamond necklace. Renee added the savings bond, which Aunt Gert received yesterday, to the large stack of bonds inside an envelope marked Savings Bonds. She put everything back inside and checked the table to be sure she hadn't forgotten anything.

Reluctantly she closed the box and lifted it to put it in its proper place. The one-carat diamond solitaire and matching wedding band flashed under the fluorescent lighting. She would have traded the ring and everything she owned for the missing necklace. She looked at the wedding band then took the box back down and opened it.

Renee slowly slid the solitaire and wedding band off her finger. Her marriage had been a sham and she should have stopped wearing the rings weeks ago. As she put the rings in the box, she wondered what it was about her that made the people she cared for abandon her.

She hadn't married Marc for love. Theirs had been a marriage of mutual interest. Marc had agreed with her belief that love develops and grows during marriage and she'd been in love with the idea of loving him. Now, she knew that was lie. He'd lied about everything. She closed the box and placed it in the empty opening in the wall.

A few minutes later, she braved the heat and walked to her car. Through the windshield, she watched the heavy, gray clouds billow and roll in the hot Birmingham sky. The dark, rolling clouds matched her mood as hurt and fear circled and expanded inside her.

"Damn him. Damn him," she said. Her voice was husky as she put the key into the ignition. The V-8 engine roared to life and she pressed the buttons on her door and lowered her windows letting the hot air escape.

Why had Marc taken the necklace? she wondered.

Marrying Marc Foster had been a mistake. She didn't mind taking responsibility for her mistakes. Hadn't she taken it like a big girl when she learned her husband of less than a year had not *one* but two other wives, Danielle Timmons Foster and Alexandria Lord-Wright Foster? Hadn't she swallowed her pride and agreed to join forces with Danielle and Alex instead of waging war like she wanted? They'd worked together to learn the truth about the man they'd married and to untangle his web of lies. During the past month, the three of them had become friends instead of enemies.

Danielle and Alex couldn't help her with this.

She'd married Marc and if he'd taken the necklace then she was partially responsible for its disappearance. It wasn't fair that her great-aunt would be hurt by her mistake.

Renee turned the air-conditioning on high, letting the rapidly cooling air blow on her face. What was she going to tell her aunt Gert?

She brushed away the tears on her cheek, leaving dark stains on the sleeve of her jacket. It was no use crying. Crying never solved anything. If it did, she would have been the girl her parents wanted her to be. She would have been the wife Marc wanted her to be.

What she needed was a plan, she thought. Renee shifted into Reverse and backed out of the parking spot. She maneuvered her way into the afternoon traffic. By the time she got on I-459, she had a sketchy outline of a plan. If she could avoid telling her great-aunt that the necklace was missing, she would. She was going to find the necklace. It was her fault it was gone in the first place. If she'd never married Marc, this wouldn't have happened. Since his death, she'd had nothing but heartache and one unpleasant surprise after another. She realized she didn't know the man she'd married but she did know her aunt Gert. Renee knew what that necklace meant to her. Marc had known it, too.

Renee pressed her lips together. Marc had hurt her but she wasn't going to let him hurt her aunt. She was going to find that necklace. One way or another she would.

June 4

The office of Smithstone & Wasson was exactly as Chris Foster had imagined: traditional, Southern and intimidating as hell. It was a good thing that he wasn't easily intimidated. Chris leaned back in the large leather chair and scanned the quiet waiting area. It wasn't a room but more like a den with leather chairs and sofas, thick brown carpet and he'd bet his salary that the furniture was antique. The place said money and a lot of it. Renee Foster hadn't scrimped when she'd sicced the junkyard dog of a lawyer on him…or rather Marc Foster's estate, he thought.

Chris rubbed his hand over his chin. His brother, Marc, had never been one to do things the easy way, even in death. He'd grieved when he'd gotten a call from the police in South Carolina telling him his older brother was dead. He hadn't seen or spoken to his brother in over two years. They hadn't been close for more than ten years but despite that Marc had been the only family he had left. Marc had become a perpetual liar. It had gotten to the point where he trusted very little Marc told him and his lies had been the major reason they had drifted apart. Chris curled his lip and brushed aside the memory.

Essentially he'd been on his own since he was fourteen. But part of him remembered his older brother who would beat the hell out of anyone who messed with him, the brother who would bring him sandwiches from the diner where he worked when there was hardly any food in the house. Those images conflicted with the selfish bastard who'd married three different women. Chris hated the situation Marc had put him in.

He could have walked away. Hell, he'd wanted to say "to hell with this" many times in the past month. But he'd given his word, and once he gave his word that was that. Now, he was in Birmingham, Alabama, to meet with Renee Foster's lawyer. They wouldn't have needed lawyers if she'd been reasonable. The estate could have been settled and he would have been out of this mess and gone on with his life.

A dark paneled door across the room opened and a young Asian woman walked out. "Mr. Foster?"

"Yes," he said and stood.

The woman smiled. "Mr. Smithstone will see you now. Please follow me."

She led him through a quiet hallway filled with paintings and other artwork. Thick carpet muffled the sound of their footsteps. He gave an inward nod of approval to the discreet cameras and motion detectors. The lawyer had hired a good security firm. He wasn't surprised.

The woman opened a door at the end of the hall and stepped into a large room where an older woman stopped typing and gave him a smile. The woman who'd led him there closed the door quietly behind them. She walked to another door and knocked twice before opening it.

Chris stepped inside and paused. A large, dark

wood conference table dominated the room, and all but two chairs stood empty in the room. Chris barely glanced at the suit, who he assumed was Terrell Smithstone; it was Renee Foster who captured his attention.

Chris kept his expression blank as he watched his brother's widow. There was nothing classically beautiful about her features. Her skin was a light brown, which reminded him of his favorite milk chocolate candy. Her eyes were dark brown and somber. She had an air of vulnerability around her that made him want to protect her. The thoughts were quickly dispelled when her lawyer stood.

"Mr. Foster. I'm Terrell Smithstone. I believe you know my client, Renee Foster."

Chris shook the man's outstretched hand, noting the rough calluses. He had the hands of a man who did manual labor, not the soft hands of a desk jockey or a lawyer. Chris would have to add that bit of information to Smithstone's file. He'd investigated Smithstone and all of Marc's wives.

Renee cleared her throat. "Terrell, would you mind if I spoke with Chris alone?" Her voice was smooth like honey. Chris mentally raised a brow at the use of Smithstone's first name and at the tone of her voice. It was a tone used with friends. He wondered how well the two knew each other.

Chris didn't like the feel of this situation. He'd worked as a special agent for the FBI for almost six years and before that he'd worked three years as a cop in California. He'd developed a radar for trouble and right about now his radar was telling him things were about to hit the fan.

"I don't think this is wise," Smithstone said. "As your attorney, I'm advising you to rethink this."

Renee folded her hands on the table and leaned forward. "I've made up my mind," she said softly.

Chris watched the interaction between the two. He didn't know what was going on but if her lawyer was against it maybe she'd decided to be reasonable. Maybe he could put this whole mess behind him.

Who the hell was he kidding? Renee Foster hadn't made a damn thing easy.

Smithstone picked up a folder on the table. "If you need me, just tell my secretary." He walked out of the room and closed the door behind him.

Chris returned his gaze to Renee.

"Please have a seat, Chris," she said, nodding to the chair on the opposite side of the table. Chris walked to the chair and sat down across from her and waited. If she was nervous, she didn't show it. Her expression was serene and carefully blank. She'd learned to hide what she was thinking and he wondered what was going on in her head.

"What do you hope to accomplish with this meeting today?" she asked.

This was a surprise, he thought. He'd made his plans clear to all three women. He wanted to settle Marc's estate in a way that was fair to everyone.

"The same thing I'd hoped to accomplish for the past month—to settle Marc's estate. Why the sudden interest?"

She held his gaze and studied him with the intensity of a starving man at a buffet. For a brief moment, he could sense the turmoil behind the polite expression. He tensed, waiting for the other shoe to drop.

Renee studied her hands, surprised they weren't shaking or clenched. She was taking a risk. A big risk. It would be worth it, she thought. It had to be.

Meeting Chris Foster again was harder than she thought it would be. He looked nothing like Marc, for which she was grateful. She didn't know if she could go through with her plan if he'd remotely resembled his brother.

She could do this, she thought. She would do this. She lifted her head and met his steady gaze. His eyes were the color of pale amber framed by long, black lashes. They reminded her of a panther she'd seen on a television documentary. The panther looked like a lazy cat but later proved that looks could be deceiving. The cat had been a dangerous and deadly predator. She hoped Chris Foster wasn't.

"I will agree to the terms of your latest offer. If…" She paused and swallowed. Her mouth felt dry and she wished she'd accepted the secretary's earlier offer to get her something to drink. "If," she continued, "you will find something Marc took from my family." Please, God, she prayed. Please let him accept this offer.

"What did Marc take?"

Renee opened the black portfolio in front of her and slid the photograph across the table. She watched as he picked up the picture and studied it. She was surprised by his lack of reaction to the photo. The picture was flawless like the diamonds in the necklace were—flawless and breathtaking.

"Real diamonds?" he asked, then put the picture on the table.

"Of course," she said. "I had the necklace appraised again for my great-aunt last year. Here are copies of two appraisals," she said and gave him a folder.

He took the folder and flipped through the pages. His brows drew together in a frown. "Are you sure Marc took it?"

"I'm positive. My great-aunt asked Marc to take it to the jeweler to have it cleaned. I usually do that for her, but this time she asked Marc to do it. The necklace was in a safe-deposit box and Marc's initials were on the release form. I've contacted all the jewelry stores in Birmingham and none of them had the necklace. I've looked through all of Marc's papers and couldn't find anything about the necklace."

"If I decide to look for the necklace, what guarantee do I have that you will keep your word?"

"I will have Terrell draft a contract. You haven't known me for long and you have no reason to trust me. I understand that. But I have no reason to trust you, either. I think a contract clearly stating the terms would be best." He seemed like a nice enough guy. He'd tried to create order at Marc's funeral when the three wives learned of each other's existence. When she saw him again on the Marc III, the yacht Marc purchased with money he'd stolen from Alex, Chris appeared to honestly want to do what was fair for all of them. Still, she had a hard time trusting him, Marc's brother, without an iron-clad contract. Marc had shown her that it was best not to trust a Foster man.

"What makes you think I can find this necklace and how long has it been missing?"

"The necklace has been gone for about a month. Why do I think you can find the necklace?" She raised her hand, lifted her index finger. "One. From what I've heard, you are good at your job. Two. You work for the FBI and you have access to more resources than a private investigator. Three. I think you want to see the last of me and my lawyer. Because if that necklace isn't returned to my aunt Gert before she finds out it's missing, I can guarantee you that I will make this process as slow and painful as possible."

"Are you threatening me?" he asked softly. His pale brown gaze hardened.

Her mouth grew dry like Weiss Lake during last year's drought. She didn't want to imagine what he could do to her if he thought she was a threat to him. Marc had been in decent shape, but this man exuded a kind of strength and power that was unmistakable.

"No. I'm not threatening you. I'm just letting you know how important it is for me to get this necklace to Aunt Gert. So do we have a deal?" she asked, hoping she didn't sound as desperate and afraid as she was. She leaned her arms on the large conference room table and linked her fingers together to keep them from shaking.

He glanced down at the picture of the necklace that he'd laid on the table in front of him. His long, black lashes concealed his gaze and should have made him look feminine, but there was nothing soft about Chris Foster. He slid the photo to the side. "I'll help you find the necklace."

"Great," she said, nearly sighing in relief. "I figured we could start with Marc's credit cards."

"We?"

"Yes, we."

"I thought the deal was for me to find the necklace."

"I *do* want you to find it, but I'm not going to sit around doing nothing."

"What do you know about recovering stolen jewelry?"

"Nothing, but I do know how to find information and how to find it quickly. This will be a joint effort. I expect you to include me and to use my skills as a research librarian. I won't be left out of the loop on this."

"I work better alone."

"Working alone isn't an option. It's all or nothing."

Chapter 2

Renee sat with her back straight and her hands resting in her lap. After years of Saturday morning etiquette and decorum classes, she was well aware of the calm and relaxed image she projected. She'd learned two important lessons from all those years of misery in classes where she just didn't fit in with the other girls: straight and erect posture and what she called her "game" face. Social etiquette didn't make sense to her. There were too many rules and too many exceptions to the rules. But learning to hide her emotions behind the game face had gotten her through the countless social events her parents forced her to attend. It had helped her hide her pain and saved her pride when her parents left her at school during the holidays. This time it wasn't just her pride at stake. Chris Foster had to accept her offer. He was her last hope.

She kept her expression calm and serene. But her stomach felt as if she'd swallowed a box of rocks. She needed his help and she hated feeling so dependent on him. If she could have found a private detective willing to find the necklace without telling her aunt Gert, she would have done everything she could to avoid coming in direct contact with Chris Foster again. The man made her nervous. He was too suave, too sexy, too charming.

To be perfectly honest, it wasn't his charm that made her nervous. It was the fact that Chris Foster was drop-dead gorgeous. Impossibly long, black eyelashes framed his golden-brown eyes. The combination was all the more disturbing now that she had his complete attention. It was as if he was searching for answers in her expression and he had all the time in the world to find them. She wanted to look away and break the connection his look had forged between them. But she couldn't afford to back away—not if she wanted to find the necklace.

"All right," he said, breaking the silence in the conference room. "We'll work together, but under my terms."

She silently sighed in relief then tilted her head to the side. The relief she felt warred with suspicion. "What terms?" She needed him, but she'd learned from her mistake with Marc to not totally trust the Foster men.

He rested his arms on the table and leaned forward.

Everything in her wanted to draw closer to him. Renee blinked. Startled by her reaction, she drew back and willed her heart rate to return somewhere close to normal. Years ago, she'd helped her friend, Karen Smithstone, gather research for her thesis on sexual chemistry. Until now, Renee had never experienced the strong sexual attraction described in Karen's paper. This was just great. Why did he have to produce pheromones that made her body ache? She didn't care how attracted she was to him. The only thing that mattered was getting the necklace back.

"First," he said, his voice firm, "we'll work together, but what *I* say goes. If I feel the situation is too dangerous for you, you're out and you're staying out."

"If you think the situation is dangerous then I'll let you handle it, but you can forget the other. This is a partnership, not a dictatorship."

"Dictatorship," he said and raised his brows. "Call it whatever you want. You don't know anything about finding stolen jewelry. Your inexperience could get us both in a tight situation or worse."

He had a point. "Fine. Teach me what I need to know, but don't expect me to blindly follow you. This necklace is too important for me to leave it entirely in someone else's hands."

"Even if the hands are more capable than yours?"

"If you're as good as I've heard, then there won't be any reason for you to worry about me. Oh, and another thing, I don't want Aunt Gert to know the necklace is missing. She's an old lady and I don't want Marc's actions to cause her pain."

He studied her and silence grew between them. Her stomach tightened with fear. She knew she was pushing her luck with him, but had she gone too far?

"If she gave Marc permission to take the necklace then I'll need to talk to her."

"Talk to her all you want, but just don't let her know the necklace is gone."

"I won't say anything to her. For now."

She felt a tinge of uneasiness. He'd qualified his statement, but she had a feeling that he would balk if she pushed him again. She'd take it because she really didn't have a choice.

"Then we have a deal." Renee held out her hand.

He grasped it. Heat seemed to smolder where their hands met. His grip was strong without being too overpowering. Unlike Marc's hands, which were fairly smooth, his hands were firm and callused. Unwilling desire sparked inside of her. It was a feeling she hadn't experienced in years. She raised her gaze to his and the heat spread quickly throughout her body. This was crazy, she thought and pulled her hand away. She didn't know what it was about Chris that made her feel this way, but she couldn't afford to think of him as anything but the man who was helping her find Aunt Gert's necklace. As handsome as he was, he was the very last man she should trust.

"Deal," he said.

It took everything within her not to sag in the chair like a Raggedy Ann doll. She'd been so afraid that he'd refuse to help her and then she'd be forced to admit to Aunt Gert that she'd brought a thief into her life.

"Great. I'll get Terrell to draw up the contract so that we can get started." For the first time in weeks, she felt as if she was finally going to get this situation straightened out.

"You don't have to do that. I give you my word that I'll look for the necklace."

"No offense, but your brother has made me question everything people have told me. I'm taking no one's word for anything. I insist on a contract between us."

His expression went from relaxed to angry. She'd always considered brown eyes as warm, but icy fury filled his golden-brown eyes. "I'm not Marc, Mrs. Foster." His voice was sharp and cold. "Send me the contract." He rose to his feet.

There was no mistaking his anger. "Too bad you're angry. You'll have to get over it. This is very important to me and it's urgent that the necklace is found quickly. I'm not taking any more chances and certainly not with you."

He looked at her coldly and picked up the photo of the necklace. "I'll get this back to you."

"Keep it." She bit the words off.

He slid the photo into an envelope and walked to the door. He turned toward her. "I'll be in touch." He opened the door and started to walk out.

"Not so fast." She stood and walked around the table. He turned toward her and held open the door.

"I expect you to call me tomorrow." She raised her chin at his frown and plowed on. "I also expect you to call me whenever you find something new. You're going to have to work in Birmingham some of the time. I have an excellent computer network in my home. I want you to work there."

He looked at her as if she'd turned into the Wicked Witch of the West. "I'll call you. Soon." His tone was cold, but his gaze even colder. He gave her a curt nod and walked out.

When the door closed, she finally let down her guard and her shoulders slumped under the weight and worry that had gripped her since learning the necklace was gone. She walked slowly to her chair and sat down. She'd gotten what she'd wanted in this meeting. She'd won the battle, but she wasn't sure she'd win the war if Chris Foster was involved. She leaned back in the chair. Now that he was gone, she realized how tense she'd been. If he made her feel this way in an office, how was she going to feel when he came to her home? Renee tightened her lips. She'd deal with it. Like she'd dealt with every unpleasant thing she'd had to deal with since Marc's death.

The door opened again and Terrell walked inside. "So do I need to draw up a contract?"

"Yes," she said and sat up straight.

"Are you sure this is what you want to do?"

She looked at her friend and lawyer. "This is what I have to do. I don't really have a choice if I want to find the necklace before Aunt Gert finds out it's gone."

"You should tell her about Marc. She'll understand. This isn't your fault."

But it was. If she hadn't married Marc, none of this would have happened. There was no way she was going to tell her what happened. Her great-aunt was the only family who cared for her and she wasn't about to lose her. She couldn't bear it if Aunt Gert treated her like her parents treated her. Renee wouldn't take that chance.

"I brought Marc into her life. I've got to make this right."

"You aren't responsible for Marc's actions. He's responsible."

She shook her head. "Let's agree to disagree."

Terrell raised one side of his mouth. "In other words, shut up and leave you alone."

Renee shrugged her shoulders and smiled. Terrell understood her. She considered him and his sister, Karen, to be her only friends. But even with them, she never really completely let down her

guard to be herself. People never wanted to see the
real Renee. They only wanted to see the precon-
ceived image, and that image couldn't be hurt.

"Hey," Terrell said. "Dad's cooking out in two
weeks and Mom said to tell you to come over
around six and bring Miss Gert."

"Okay, but I'll have to check with Aunt Gert.
She's usually busy on the weekends."

He shook his head. "I thought people slowed
down when they got older."

"Try explaining that to Aunt Gert."

Renee called Alex when she arrived home. She'd
been so busy contacting the jewelry stores in Birmingham trying to locate the necklace that she hadn't
thought to ask Alex or Danielle if they had it.

Alex was the youngest of the three women Marc
had married. Because of her wealth and past party-
girl lifestyle, she hadn't taken Alex seriously when
they'd first met. That had changed. She'd learned
over the last few weeks that Alex had a generous
heart and a fine business mind.

Alex and Chris's friend, Hunter Smith, had
worked together to recover the millions Marc had
embezzled from Alex's family business.

"Renee, I'm so glad you called. I was going to
call you and Danielle tonight," Alex said.

"Well, you can tell us now. Hang on. I'm going
to add Danielle." Danielle owned half of a large
shipping company that her brother and his best

friend, Tristan Adams, started before her brother's death in Iraq. She'd been married to Marc the longest and was a former model.

"Hello, everyone," Danielle said.

"I'm so excited. I've got good news," Alex said.

"Well, tell us," Renee said, needing some good news today.

"Hunter and I are getting married."

"That's wonderful," Danielle said.

"Congratulations. I'm so glad everything worked out," Renee said.

She and Danielle could see that Hunter had deep feelings for Alex when they were all on the yacht. They'd encouraged Alex to take a chance and to not let what happened with Marc stop her from finding love with Hunter.

"Oh, thank you. Little Sweetie and I are so happy and I want both of you to come to my wedding," Alex said.

Renee smiled. Little Sweetie was Alex's pampered Chihuahua whom she'd brought with her to Marc's funeral.

"When are you getting married?" Danielle asked.

"We're having a small ceremony on the yacht in two weeks," Alex said.

"Two weeks?" Renee asked, surprised.

"I know it's short notice but there's no reason to wait," Alex said.

"I'll be there," Danielle said.

"So will I, Alex," Renee added.

"Oh, good. Having the two of you there will mean a lot to me," Alex said. "Oh, but, Renee, you called me. What did you want to talk to us about?"

"I wanted to know if Marc gave you diamond jewelry other than your wedding ring," Renee asked and waited anxiously for their response.

"No," Danielle said.

"Me, either. Why?" Alex asked.

"I'm trying to find a piece of jewelry and I wondered if Marc had given it to you, but I guess he didn't," Renee replied. It had been worth a try.

"I'm sorry," Alex said. Renee could hear the sadness in her voice.

"Don't worry about it, Alex. You've got a wedding to plan. What do you wear to a wedding on a yacht?" Renee asked. She didn't want bad news to spoil Alex's announcement. She would tell them about Aunt Gert's necklace after the wedding.

They yielded to Danielle, who'd been a fashion model and agreed to wear a nice dress before they ended the call.

Later that evening she'd placed two chocolate cakes on wire racks to cool when her cell phone rang. She wiped her hands on the vintage apron and removed the phone from the pocket of her skirt. She looked at the number on the screen and steadied herself.

"Hi, Aunt Gert. How was your day?" Aunt Gert and five of her friends had hired a van and a driver to take them to the casinos in Mississippi. She'd told her great-aunt that Marc had a younger brother and she was meeting with him about Marc's estate. It was mostly the truth and would explain the time she'd have to spend with Chris Foster.

"Never mind about that. Tell me, how did your meeting with Marc's brother go today?" Aunt Gert asked, her voice brimming with curiosity.

So much for stalling, she thought. She'd been expecting the question all evening. Aunt Gert had to be the nosiest person in the world. The older she got the more personal and blunt her questions became. She'd tried to get her to tone down her questions, but Aunt Gert had said to her, "I'm too darn old to be beating around the bush. If I want to know something I'm just going to ask."

"It went fine. Both of us want to settle Marc's estate as quickly as possible." Okay, *Chris* wanted to settle the estate quickly and she wanted the necklace.

"So are you okay financially? Marc didn't leave you in debt like Mrs. Hutton's husband left her?"

"Oh, no, ma'am. There are just a couple of loose ends to finalize."

"What kind of loose ends, and did you find out why Marc never told you he had a brother?"

Leave it to her aunt to get straight to the point. She wished she could tell her the truth and remove the weight of Marc's betrayal from her shoulders. But she couldn't. She was too afraid she'd lose the one person who hadn't let her down, who hadn't left her. "I don't think they were close. He's Marc's younger brother."

"They must have been close at some point for Marc to make him the executor."

"I guess so." Renee sighed. "At this point, I just want this whole thing over with."

"I know you do, sweet girl." Her tone softened. "You know if you need me, I'll come back."

"No. Don't cut your trip short. I have got everything under control."

"You don't have to do everything yourself."

"I'm not. Terrell is doing a great job of representing my best interests."

"I'm sure he is. I'll be back home next week. If there's anything you want me to do just let me know."

"I will, Aunt Gert."

"Hmm. No you won't. I'll have to invite myself to do something, then you won't have a choice but to let me help."

Renee laughed. "I promise to let you help me."

"See that you do. Love you much, Renee. I'll talk to you later."

"Good night." Renee hit the off button and put the phone back in her pocket. She'd gotten off easy tonight. Usually Aunt Gert was focused when it came to asking questions and she had a lot of questions about Marc. Questions Renee couldn't answer without risking Aunt Gert's love. She didn't know what it was about her that made her parents not love her. She'd spent years trying to be the kind of daughter they would love and in the end nothing she did made a difference. Aunt Gert loved the image she presented to the world and Renee had worked hard to never reveal her true self because no one loved the real Renee.

Gertrude Mitchell placed the cell phone on the nightstand and frowned.

"How's Renee?"

Gert looked at the man she'd loved for most of her life. He lay back against the mound of extra pillows he always requested when they were together. He looked nothing like the bold young man she'd fallen in love with in New York. The doctors in Switzerland had done an excellent job of transforming gangster Ike "Big Ike" Henderson into now-retired business-man Dean Benson. They'd given him a new face, but the eyes were the same. Gert laid her head on his shoulder, enjoying the scent that was truly his own.

"Something's bothering her and she's trying hard to pretend everything is okay."

"Is something going on with Marc's estate?" He ran his hand along her shoulder.

"I don't know if it's Marc's estate or Marc." She placed her hand on his chest, indulging in the cool feel of the black silk robe. "Whatever it is, I'm go-ing to make sure she doesn't face this alone. You can best believe her selfish, no-good parents aren't going to help her."

He kissed her brow. "She's lucky that she has you."

"Yes, she is, and I'm lucky to have her. She deserves to be happy."

"Wasn't she happy with Marc?"

"I don't think so. I know this business with the estate isn't making her happy."

"We'll find a way to help her get through this."

"I know." She closed her eyes and enjoyed being held in his arms. They didn't have much time left to spend together. He had an early-morning flight to his home in Switzerland tomorrow. "You will come to the dance in a few weeks, won't you?"

He tightened his arms around her. "I'll be at the dance. I want to see you wearing the necklace again."

"I'll wear it just for you." Gert smiled and kissed his chin. She'd ask Renee to get the necklace from her safe deposit box before the dance. Her thoughts returned to her conversation with Renee.

Gert smiled and kissed his chin. One way or another she would find out what was bothering Renee.

Chapter 3

Renee looked at the Victorian-style clock that sep-arated the biology and botany sections of the book-shelf across the room. At eight-thirty most Saturday mornings, she would still be in her pajamas and enjoying her first cup of coffee. Today, she had been awake since six o'clock, unable to sleep a minute longer. Chris Foster was coming to Birm-ingham to begin looking for the necklace. She'd been standing at the window waiting for a car to park in front of the house for the past five minutes. There was nothing else for her to do but wait.

She wanted to call and find out his exact location, but she could not bring herself to do it.

"He'll be here," she whispered. She turned back to the window. There was no reason for him to not show up. There'd been no reason for her parents not to show up at her school, either, but they hadn't on so many occasions that she'd stopped expecting them by the time she was in the seventh grade. Unlike her parents, he had an incentive to come here.

He wanted to settle Marc's estate as much as she wanted to find Aunt Gert's necklace.

She'd spent every minute of her free time trying to put together all the information she could find on Marc's travels for the last year. Renee, Danielle and Alex decided to work together and track his movements in hopes of trying to rectify the havoc Marc had played in their lives. Alex was missing about a million dollars that Marc had taken from her family's business and her personal accounts. He'd taken the opportunity to have children with Danielle, and he'd taken Aunt Gert's necklace from her.

Marc Foster had a lot to answer for. The anger she'd thought she'd released by beating the living daylights out of bread dough this morning still bubbled inside her. Every time she thought about Marc, she wanted to punch something. Yoga and meditation weren't helping to release the rage she felt when she imagined how hurt Aunt Gert would be if she learned her necklace had been stolen.

Renee unclenched her hands and rubbed them on her black cotton pants. Getting mad wasn't going to help. She left the window and walked across the thick rug to one of the sections of the wall-to-wall bookshelves.

She moved a book a quarter of an inch forward to line up with the rest of the books on the shelf. She couldn't believe how anxious she was to have Chris in her home. With a sigh, she glanced at the clock again. Punctuality hadn't been Marc's strong suit. Neither had fidelity or truthfulness.

She tugged on the hem of her white cotton blouse that was still crisp and wrinkle free. It wouldn't remain that way. No matter how hard she tried, her clothes ended up wrinkled or stained by the end of the day. One thing her parents had drilled into her was that appearances mattered, which was why they'd been so disappointed with her. Renee wasn't the beautiful, socially adept child they'd tried to mold her to be. Instead they got an awkward child who was more interested in books and learning to cook than looking pretty on demand. She'd spent years trying to please her parents. Marc had accepted her for herself, or he'd pretended to accept her.

She could feel herself getting angrier just thinking about the way he'd lied to her just like her parents had lied when they said they were going to visit her in school. They never had. Renee walked across the room to a chair, slipped off her black clogs and sat down. She closed her eyes and tried to enter into her "peaceful" place, but peace was hard to find when you wanted to strangle someone who was already dead. After a minute she gave up and opened her eyes. She reached for the book on the table. Meditation wasn't helping her to relax…maybe the latest murder mystery would.

Chris put his Explorer in Park and lowered his window. He didn't need to check the address because he'd made a point of learning exactly where Renee lived on his last trip to Birmingham. The large, white Victorian house was unexpected. He knew she and Marc had lived in a condo in downtown Birmingham and as of yesterday, she still owned that property. He'd driven down several streets with rows of Victorian-style homes on large lots and sidewalks on either side of the street on the way here. Chris got out of the car. The sound of children laughing drifted from the backyard a few houses down.

This neighborhood was a long way from the falling-apart houses and apartments where he and Marc grew up. It was the kind of house a kid like him had dreamed of living in. How different would his life have been if he'd lived here? He shrugged then reached inside the car and grabbed his briefcase and a box of Marc's possessions. That was the past. Now, home was wherever his next assignment took him. No strings. No obligations. No ties. Only the next assignment, or in this case, where his promise to Marc took him.

Heat enveloped him as he walked up the front walkway that was lined with a straight row of bushes thick with small, white flowers. As he climbed the short flight of stairs to the wraparound porch, he could smell the sweet scent of the flowers.

When he reached the door, he rang the doorbell and waited under the cooler shade of the porch. The cement floor had been painted the color of the reddish-brown Birmingham soil. A green mat in front of the door spelled Welcome in black letters. He waited a moment then rang the bell again. She couldn't have forgotten that he was coming, of that he was sure. She'd even sent him an e-mail verifying the date and time of their meeting. The front door was solid and for her sake he was glad. Doors with fancy glass were pretty, but provided little protection if someone was trying to break in.

A few seconds later, Chris walked to the windows on the left. Heavy curtains blocked the view inside. He moved to the windows on the other side of the house and cupped a hand over his eyes. The lace curtains might as well have not been there for all the good they were doing. Four froufrou girly chairs were grouped together. In one of those chairs sat Renee Foster. She sat with one foot beneath her knee and the other leg swung lazily. Her pant leg bunched at the knee revealing her calf. A pair of geriatric black shoes sat at attention beside the chair. His gaze went to the bright blue nail polish on her feet.

She had the prettiest feet he'd ever seen. If they were as soft and smooth as they looked, why in the hell did she hide them in shoes that were just plain ugly? It made him wonder what else she was hiding. He let his gaze follow the arch of her foot, to her ankle and up the smooth curve of her calf. He felt a pull of desire and heat that had nothing to do with the summer weather. What the hell was wrong with him? All she was doing was reading a book and showing her calf and he was acting like she'd offered to strip naked for him.

"Hell, Foster. Get a grip," he muttered. She was off-limits. Way off-limits. Chris rapped hard on the window. "Just find the damn necklace and get back to Atlanta." He knocked harder, making the glass rattle from the force. She blinked as if coming awake after a long night's sleep. She stared at him as if she didn't recognize him for a second. Then color flooded her cheeks. He watched as she put the book facedown on the armrest and mouthed, "Be right there."

Chris watched as she walked out of the room. Her black pants outlined the shape of her rear. He stood, enjoying the sway of her hips. If things were different he'd make a point of getting to know this woman. But things weren't different. He turned from the window and walked to the door.

She opened the door and gestured him inside. "I'm so sorry. I didn't hear the bell. I hope you weren't waiting long."

He stepped inside the foyer. Sunlight streamed in from a large second-story window and the sweet smell of chocolate reminded him of his favorite bakery in Los Angeles. He hoped she'd offer him a sample of whatever it was she'd baked. If it was as good as it smelled, it might make up for him leaving his apartment so early in the morning.

"I didn't wait long," he said. "You seemed to be really into your book. Do you always get so involved in your book that you don't hear the doorbell?"

She closed the door and he saw the faint hint of color in her cheeks. "Not always, but I can pretty much tunc out anything when I really get involved with a book. Do you want anything before we get started?"

Not really, but if getting a drink would get things started he'd take one. He shifted the box and nearly dropped it. "I'll take anything cold."

"Let me take your briefcase," she said, reaching for the battered leather case.

Their hands touched briefly, but he could feel the touch as if he'd been branded. Only years of training kept him from jerking his hand away. She walked to the door opposite the library and opened it. "We'll do most of our work in my office."

Chris whistled low and long when he stepped inside. Her office was more like a computer lab. He counted at least five computers and various other types of equipment stacked on racks—lights flashed and blinked. All of the equipment looked brand-new. "I can see why you have your curtains closed for this room."

"I like to play with my computers."

He raised a brow and looked at her. "This is more than playing."

"It's not really," she said, placing his briefcase on one of the desks. "I'm going to get something to drink before we get started. What would you like? I've got Coke, sweet tea, lemonade, ginger ale and water."

"Tea's fine."

"I'll be right back." She turned and hurried out the door. He placed the box on the desk beside his briefcase and walked to a rack on the opposite side of the room. He knew enough about computers to know that Renee didn't "play" with these computers. The equipment looked like top-of-the-line stuff.

When she'd mentioned her computer network, he thought she meant she had a relatively new home computer network. What he saw here was above and beyond the average home setup. There was nothing in her background check that mentioned her skill with computers. Math and library science—yes. If she was so good with computers why didn't she work in that field? This bit of information played hell with him. Like the blue nail polish. He was beginning to think there was more to Renee Foster.

He turned when he heard her footsteps. She carried a good-size metal tray loaded with a pitcher of tea, two glasses and a plate of cookies. "Here, let me help you with that," he said. He took the tray and set it down on the desk next to his briefcase. "You didn't have to do this."

"It's no trouble. Besides, I figure we'll need it. I hope you like chocolate pecan cookies."

Chris felt his mouth water. "What's not to like?" He reached for a cookie and bit into it. The cookie tasted like chocolate-covered sin. "This is good. Really good."

"I'm glad you like them," she said and smiled. It was the first time she'd really smiled at him. He was surprised how much he wanted her to remain smiling. *Keep your mind on the job, Foster.*

"The recipe makes three dozen so feel free to eat as many as you'd like," she continued.

Chris looked at the stack of cookies on the plate and wondered how she would react if he told her he wanted something more than cookies.

"Thanks," he said. "I am curious why a librarian has a network like this in her home."

"I have a graduate degree in Information Science. Most people get jobs as librarians with that degree, but you can also get a computer specialization with an Information Science degree. After all, a library catalog is just one big computer database," Renee said.

He relaxed a little at her explanation.

He opened his briefcase and took out his laptop and the file he'd started on his brother. The file wasn't as complete as he wanted it to be, but he

figured he could get more information from Renee
and the other wives to help fill in the gaps.

"Let's start looking for the necklace." The sooner
it was found the better for him. He picked up
another cookie on the tray and bit into it.

"Okay," Renee said. She walked to the computer
cart and rolled it next to the desk beside his. On top
of the cart sat a wide-screen laptop that made his
laptop look like a relic. Three thick black notebooks
lay on the shelf below. She put the laptop on the desk.

Chris got another cookie and opened his file.
"I've checked with agents in Los Angeles, New
York, Miami and Houston. None of their contacts
have seen the necklace."

She gave him a puzzled look. "Is that good or
bad?"

"Good because that means the necklace hasn't
been fenced through the major jewel laundering
hubs in the States. The stones are sometimes removed and sold or used to make other jewelry." He
bit into the cookie and put it down on the open
folder.

"Oh, no," she said, her eyes wide and filled with
fear. "You don't think that's what happened, do
you?"

"No. If the necklace had gone to any of those lo-
cations, someone would have let it slip and Marc
didn't have ties to gangs or organized crime. My
guess is he either sold the necklace to an individual
or he took the necklace to another jeweler to be

cleaned." He removed a page from the stack. "This is a list of commercial and smaller flights Marc took during the last month," he said, putting the paper on the desk in front of her.

She slid the paper closer and studied it. Her hands looked soft and delicate. He wondered how they would feel on his bare chest.

"This looks right," she said, then picked up one of the black notebooks on the cart. "I asked Alex and Danielle if they could track Marc's travels on their end and I created a travel calendar."

He took the calendar and compared it to his information. It was an exact match. His gut twisted in a knot. Chris looked at her. Hard. "How did you get this information?"

She looked at the calendar and then back at him and frowned. "I just told you. I got information from the other wives and added it together with my information."

The look she gave him said she was confused by his question. He was damn confused as to how she'd found information that had been difficult for him to find.

He folded his arms across his chest. "Not all of those flights were booked under Marc's name," he said softly. He'd found the information in some of Marc's possessions from the crash, but most of the information came from sources available to law enforcement and government officials. Renee was neither.

"Yes, I know. I found out that Marc had several credit cards he used under different names and addresses."

She passed along the information as if she were telling him Marc's favorite color, not like she'd just revealed that her husband had committed yet another crime.

"And you learned this how?"

"Oh, easy. Marc didn't know there was monitoring software on our computer network at home. The software recorded everything he did. Once I had credit card numbers, it was easy to find out the rest. You just need access to the right database."

Chris leaned back in the chair. Playing with computers. *Accessing the right database, my ass.* He didn't know who she thought she was fooling, but it wasn't him. He'd have to dig deeper into Renee's background. The computers in this office combined with her ability to get that kind of information on Marc said loud and clear that Renee was more than a librarian. He made a mental note to contact a librarian at the FBI Library in Quantico to find out if Renee's story was feasible. "Which credit cards did you find?"

"I found three so far," she said, flipping through the notebook. "But I've only searched the last four months, so there may be more."

There were more, but he wasn't going to share that with her just yet. She seemed to get more than enough information on her own. "What was the date that Marc took the necklace from the bank?"

"It was March 28."

"During that time, Marc had been to at least fifteen different cities. We need to contact jewelers in the area and see if anyone has seen the necklace."

"I can get a list of all of the jewelers in those cities," Renee said.

"That's good, but it would help to see anything Marc left at your old home. Did he leave any papers, notes or clothing? Did he make calls?"

"I don't know about phone calls. He didn't leave much. I put all of his things in boxes after he died. I brought them from the garage this morning," she said and pointed to the far corner of the room. "They're over there."

Chris looked at the two large cardboard boxes. It looked as if Marc traveled light like him. It was a lesson they'd had to learn as boys and neither of them had gotten out of the habit. Chris stood and walked to the corner where the boxes sat. A label with Marc's Clothing was neatly printed on top. He assumed it was Renee's writing because Marc's handwriting was sloppy and barely legible.

He took out his pocketknife and quickly cut the heavy-duty brown tape. The knife was within legal length limits in most states, but it was razor sharp at all times. This knife had saved his butt a few times in the past so he made sure it was always sharp. He slid the blade back into place and opened the box.

A crisp, white dress shirt lay on top. Chris felt nothing but sadness that this was as close as he would come to his brother ever again. He didn't know why it bothered him. They hadn't been close since they were boys. As adults, they couldn't have been more different. He lived his life with justice and honor. Marc broke the law when it suited him. It didn't matter to him who he hurt.

Chris pushed those thoughts aside. What mattered was the job and he would do it properly. He picked up the shirt and checked the pocket. It was empty. Unperturbed, he checked the seams along the bottom, then the cuffs of each sleeve.

"What are you doing?" Renee asked and came to his side.

"Checking to see if Marc had anything sewn into the seams of his shirt," he said as he guided his fingers along a side seam.

"People do that?" she said, picking up one of the sleeves.

Chris smiled at her amazed tone. "Yes."

"That's good to know," she said.

What the hell? Chris turned and looked at her. A frown wrinkled her brow as she fingered the seams of the sleeve with the focus of a sniper with a target in sight. He couldn't just let her comment pass. "Why is that good to know?"

"I have a friend who designs computer games

and he's always looking for new twists to add to the games."

"I see," he said and moved to put the shirt to the side, but Renee had a sleeve. He let go of the shirt when he realized that she wasn't going to let it go.

"What kind of things do you find in clothes?"

"Jewelry, drugs, money," he said and picked up a jacket. "Anything."

"You don't think he put the necklace in his clothing, do you?"

"I don't know. If he didn't, maybe he hid something that could point us to what he did do with the necklace."

Renee shook her head. "I just don't see Marc being the kind of guy to sew something in his clothes. He couldn't even sew on a button."

Chris raised his brow. "Marc knew how to sew."

"What do you mean? He took his clothes to the tailor if a button fell off."

"I mean we both had to learn to sew a seam and repair our clothes. We didn't have enough money growing up to throw away anything."

"So he lied about that, too."

"Yes, he did." Chris wished he'd kept his mouth closed. He could see that this information hurt her. It was just one more mess Marc made that he'd have to clean up. Chris moved his hand along the hem of the jacket and felt something hard. The kick of satisfaction had him reaching for his knife again.

Chapter 4

Chris wasn't surprised to see the gold credit card and Florida driver's license in Marc's jacket. He'd bet that Marc's other identification and credit cards were sewn into clothing and hanging in the closets of houses in Florida and Georgia. His older brother had learned to be careful. He would have had to be or else he would have made a mistake with one of the wives. Marc's life had been a balancing act and he'd been a very good juggler.

Chris put the cards down on the table. He reached for another jacket from the box and out of the corner of his eye, he saw Renee pick up the license. She hadn't believed that he'd find anything in Marc's clothing if her shocked expression was any indication. He felt sorry for her and the other wives. Marc had snowed all of them. Chris slid his fingers along the shoulder of the jacket. The sleek silk-blend fabric felt cool and smooth to the touch. No lumps or budges disrupted the tailored lines. The best thing he could do for all of them would be to settle Marc's estate and let them get on with their lives. But first, he had to figure out what happened to the necklace. He also had to figure out Renee. He shifted his position so that he could watch her without being obvious.

She studied the license as if it were a treasure map with the location of the necklace printed on it. She bit her bottom lip, which looked plump and lush like a ripe plum. He wondered if she tasted just as sweet.

Chris tightened his jaw and took his gaze from the tempting sight. Focus on the damn job, he told himself. He finished searching the jacket and laid it on top of the growing pile of clothing that had been searched.

"Did you have a flight to Florida listed at all?" she asked.

He picked up a shirt. "I don't think so. Why?"

She turned the license toward him. "This was issued in March—a month before he died. How did he get to Florida?"

He scanned the card and found the issue date. "He could have driven or taken the bus."

She shook her head. "Taking the bus doesn't sound like Marc. He always booked first-class or business-class tickets for the plane. There's not an equivalent for the bus."

"Hmm." He didn't tell her that he'd learned Marc has taken the bus one-way from Charleston to Savannah. From Savannah, he'd taken a commercial flight to Birmingham. He'd tracked down that information from a credit card that none of the wives knew he had.

"I'd better make a note to check his card records for gas charges." She walked to the cart with her laptop and began typing.

Chris continued his search of Marc's clothing. If she was lucky, she might find the information, but Marc could have used cash. She probably wouldn't find anything because cash rarely left a trail. He continued to search through Marc's clothing until the box was empty. He glanced over his shoulder at Renee. She'd pulled one of the black mesh office chairs over the to cart and her fingers moved quickly across the keys of the laptop.

He got his knife and cut open the next box. With her distracted, he could search without interruption.

This box was smaller than the other. He pulled out packing paper and reached for the brown leather organizer and flipped it over. Marc's name was printed on a small brass plate on the front. Why did Marc have a BlackBerry and this? Chris opened the organizer and began looking through the calendar. Marc's handwriting was just as sloppy as he remembered. Every day in January Marc had written at least one notation. Some entries were easy to recognize, like meetings and presentations, but others weren't. He turned the page to the next month and the next until he came to the month that Marc died. The entry made no sense to him. GMALNL-ALNYER. He'd have to look through Marc's files later to check if he'd listed anyone with the last name of Nyer. He put the planner on the desk next to the credit card and license. He would take it with him to the hotel tonight where he could access more information on his computer.

Chris looked at the computer equipment scattered around the room. He wasn't sure whether he could trust her network. Until he learned the exact extent of her computer's abilities to spy on his activities, he would search through all of Marc's things here then use the secure terminal from his hotel room to try to access the files on the external hard drive recovered from Marc's plane.

He went through the rest of the items in the box, looking for anything useful, but came up empty-handed. "Is this everything?" he asked, folding the lid of the box closed.

"That's all that was left," she replied.

"Left." Chris turned and grew silent. She'd put on a pair of black-rimmed Catwoman glasses and the staccato sound of her fingers hitting the keyboard drowned out the steady hum of computers. She should have looked ridiculous, but instead she looked bookish and sexy as she stared at the computer monitor. She was the last woman he should feel attracted to, but he couldn't deny the gut-level desire he felt. He'd had enough of Marc's hand-me-downs in his life. There was no way in hell he was going play second string to Marc's widow. He'd do what he'd done all through childhood and ignore what he couldn't have. "What do you mean?"

She looked up from the monitor and frowned. "Well." She pushed the glasses onto the bridge of her nose. "Marc had other things, but he must have taken them with him on his last trip."

"What things?"

"His briefcase, BlackBerry, the external hard drive I gave him for his birthday."

"You gave him an external hard drive as a birthday present?"

"Yes. He was always losing his jump drives. I figured he'd have a hard time losing a hard drive."

He'd never heard of a woman giving her husband a hard drive as a birthday present. What kind of relationship did they have? No. Their relationship didn't matter. What mattered was finding that necklace. Chris walked to the desk where she'd placed his briefcase and pulled out a notepad and a pen. He made a list of the missing items. The briefcase, the BlackBerry and an external hard drive were found in the wreckage. "Did he have more than one?"

"No. It was bigger than the hard drive on his laptop and he used it for backup. Once I showed him how to use it."

Chris put the notepad down. He didn't see the need to tell her about the other external hard drive that was found in Marc's plane. There was no telling how many more of Marc's secrets were waiting to explode like land mines in an abandoned field.

"I'll find out if there are any charges on the credit card and check out the driver's license. In the meantime, I need to check to see if the information you have fills in the gaps in my timeline of Marc's whereabouts." He didn't think he'd find new information, but he had to check.

"What can I do to help?"

"You can go through Marc's bank records and credit cards. Make a list of any jewelry stores he used in the last six months and make a list of names or businesses you don't recognize."

"Why the ones I don't recognize?"

"He would have had to deal with people or companies that you wouldn't be involved in. He wouldn't risk you finding out about the necklace."

She gave him a brisk nod and began typing.

He raised his eyebrows. She was actually going to do what he asked? Not wanting to give her any reason to change her mind, Chris walked to the desk and opened the briefcase. He removed his laptop and turned it on. The timeline he'd created for Marc was riddled with gaps. His brother seemed to like to disappear for a few days and so far Chris had not been able to fill them.

It didn't take him long to go through the information she'd found. Just as he'd suspected, he didn't find anything new. Chris turned and looked at her.

Half a cookie sat on a plate beside her mouse pad. Her eyes narrowed as she studied the computer screen. She looked totally engrossed in her work.

"Did you find anything?" she asked without ever looking away from the screen.

Not so engrossed after all. "No. Did you?"

"I found two jewelry stores and three names I don't recognize."

"Are the stores local?"

"Yes."

"Good. I'll head over later. I know you contacted the jewelry stores in the area to see if any of them had the necklace, but Marc might have spoken with someone about it."

She stopped typing and gave him a hard look. "*We'll* go there later."

He leaned back in the chair. "We'll head to the stores later. Are you looking at bank statements or credit card bills?"

Her expression brightened and she picked up the cookie. "Bank statements." She took a bite.

He felt a zing of desire spread throughout his body. What was it about her that attracted him so much? There were more beautiful women in the world. He should know because he'd dated a few of them. None of them had made him feel this visceral desire. His gaze focused on her lips, lush and tempting.

Chris jerked back to face his laptop. He was going to have to get himself under control. She was off-limits to him and he knew how to walk away from things he wanted. He'd had a lifetime of experience.

"I'll go through the credit cards." His voice was rough. He took a sip of the sweet tea.

"I've got some of his credit card information here." She wrinkled her nose. "I haven't looked at the statements. I can e-mail you the files."

There wasn't a chance in hell that he was going to get on her Internet connection. He reached inside his briefcase and removed his jump drive. "Just put it on this."

He rolled his chair the short distance to her desk and gave her the device. He ignored the slow burn of desire when their hands touched. He rolled his chair back to his desk.

He went to work on the credit card statements he'd retrieved a week ago. Marc hadn't denied himself any luxury. He'd purchased several Hugo Boss suits, two Rolex watches and ordered three pairs of handmade Italian shoes. His spending habits were in sharp contrast to Renee's. She bought books and a lot of them.

He turned to her. "Did you buy books for Marc?"

She looked up. "Yes, but he wasn't much of a book reader. He liked magazines and newspapers."

"There weren't any books in the boxes."

"No, they are in the library."

"You gave the books to the library?"

"No, the library in the house."

"I need to see the books."

"Okay, hold on a second." She made a few key-strokes before standing. "It's right across the hall."

He followed her out of the room and across the hall to a set of pocket doors. She pulled a latch and pushed the doors open. Each of the walls housed floor-to-ceiling bookcases filled with books. A wrought-iron rolling ladder rested in the far right corner of the room. An iron railing system connected the bookcases together. He hadn't seen this many books outside of the library.

"Did you buy all of these books?"

"No. Aunt Gert gave me some of them, but I bought most of them." She went to one of the bookcases to his left and kneeled on the hardwood floor.

As he walked farther into the room, he noticed the bookcases were built into the wall and gave an illusion of wall-to-wall bookcases. There were two large windows that let in the morning sunlight, which brought out the brownish tint to Renee's hair. She began stacking books on the floor in a neat pile.

Chris bent down. "Are these all of them?" he asked.

"Oh, no. Those are just the business books. The fiction section is over there." She pointed the opposite wall.

"You group your books?"

She looked at him over the top of her glasses. Her expression said, *I know you didn't just ask that stupid question.* He bit back a smile. She reminded him of an insulted, slightly nerdy Tinkerbell.

"Yes. I group my books. It's called cataloging. It's what librarians do."

"Sorry." The smile he'd been holding back broke through. He found her smart mouth a funny juxtaposition to the geeky glasses and loose-fitting clothes she wore. "You're the only librarian I know."

She shook her head and began to rise from her kneeling position. He stood then took her arm and helped her to her feet. Her arm felt slender, delicate and warm.

"Thanks," she said and stepped away from him.

He watched her walk quickly to the other side of the room. She'd gotten as far away from him without actually leaving the room. What was with that? He looked down at the stack of books she'd left on the floor and picked them up. He put the books on a small table. He looked at the title of the first book. It was a popular business title that he'd wanted to read. He flipped opened the book and scanned the first few pages before laying the book flat on the desk.

"Is this book new?" He flipped to the next page.
She turned around. "Which book?"

He held it up.

"No, I gave him that book about six months ago."

Chris looked at the cover. It was pristine. It didn't
look like Marc even read it. He put the book on the
desk and began flipping through each page.

"What are you looking for?" She put a large
stack of paperback books on the desk.

"Anything Marc put inside. He would hide small
things in his books when we were boys."

"Oh. What kind of things? People are constantly
leaving papers inside library books. I found a fifty-
dollar bill inside a book."

He raised a brow. "What did you do with the
money?"

She shrugged her shoulders. "Any money we
find goes into lost and found. Most of the time, it
isn't claimed and the library deposits the money
after a year."

"Couldn't you see who was the last person to
check out the book?"

"No. Once something's checked in, it's taken off
their record to protect their privacy and to keep
from clogging up the computer system with old
data."

"You weren't tempted to keep the money?" He
turned another page in the book.

"No. It wasn't my money."

Was she serious? Marc would have pocketed the

money without even thinking about it. He watched her thumb through the pages of one of the paperbacks. How in the world had his brother ended up married to her?

He removed the book jacket then put it back on when he found nothing and set that book aside.

"So what did he hide in his books?"

Chris reached for another hardback. "Money, papers, his report cards when he had bad grades."

"How do you know this?"

"I was a typical younger brother wanting what my big brother had. I would go through his stuff when he wasn't home." He smiled at the horrified look on her face.

"That's just wrong." She frowned at him.

"No, it's not. It's what brothers and sisters do to each other. Marc did the same thing with my stuff all the time."

"Why?"

He shrugged his shoulders. "Curiosity or to get back at me for something I did to him."

"That just doesn't make any sense." She picked up another book and flipped through the pages.

"I guess it wouldn't make sense to an only child." He turned a page. Between the pages lay a receipt. He picked it up. "Do you shop at H. Morgan and Sons Jewelers?"

"No, but that's where I take Aunt Gert's necklace to be cleaned." She walked around the desk. "Did you find something?"

"This is a receipt for a diamond necklace he bought the month he died." He tilted his head. "Do you know anything about it?" For a brief moment he saw a flash of hurt in her eyes. He knew the answer before she responded.

She shook her head and began rearranging the books on the table. "He didn't buy it for me."

This was a hell of a situation. "I'm sorry." The words seemed pitiful and inadequate. He'd thought of her as a pain in the butt with her constant refusal to accept his offers to settle Marc's estate. To him, it was just another bad situation his brother had dragged him into. He'd been sure she was being difficult to get back at Marc through him, but she looked really hurt.

She looked up. "Thank you." Her voice was quiet.

"You're welcome." He picked up the last hardback book. He'd known Marc's actions hurt the women he'd married, but it was another thing to see that hurt up close and personal. She couldn't fake the kind of pain he'd seen on her face. He quickly searched the book and watched as she closed the covers of the last paperback. Something softened inside him. She was not only a victim of a crime; she'd been totally betrayed by Marc. This was yet another one of his lies. "Look. I don't know why Marc acted the way he did. But you can't let his actions continue to hurt you."

She gave him a smile tinged with sadness. "It's hard not to be hurt when your husband buys jewelry for another woman."

He rubbed the back of his neck. "I know. There was something wrong with Marc, not you. You loved him, but I don't think Marc knew how to love anybody."

Her dark brown gaze met his. "I didn't love Marc."

He dropped his hand to his side. He couldn't have heard her correctly.

The doorbell rang, interrupting his thoughts. She walked out of the room. He followed to the door of the library and watched as she opened the door. Standing on the other side were two little girls. They had the same facial features so he assumed the taller one was the older sister of the smaller girl who looked to be on the verge of tears.

"Hi, Miss Renee," the older girl said and smiled, displaying a gap in her grin from a missing front tooth.

"Hello, Brandy, Brittany."

The little girl muttered "hello" then quickly lowered her head.

"Brittany's group in the community center is selling candy and she's supposed to ask you if you'd like to buy some and I'm supposed to let her ask you herself and just stand here so she won't be so scared. Go ahead, Brittany. Ask her." She nudged Brittany forward.

Chris bit back a smile at the mile-a-minute spiel.

Renee bent down on her knee in front of a clearly reluctant girl. "Did you want to ask me something, Brittany?" she asked softly.

The girl nodded her head, looked up at Renee's smiling face. A few seconds later, Brittany lifted a brochure an inch from Renee's nose and said in a trembling, small voice, "Do you want to buy candy?"

Renee gently took the brochure from the girl and made a big show of looking it over.

"They got chocolate and caramel and peanut butter," Brandy said.

"So I see," Renee said. "I think I'll have one of each, Brittany." She turned over the brochure. "Am I supposed to put my name here?"

Brittany nodded and held out a pen. Renee took the pen and wrote on the back. "Wait here and let me get the money." She straightened then walked across the hall to the office.

"See," he heard Brandy say. "I told you Miss Renee was nice. She bought three boxes of candy so you don't have to sell any more."

Chris watched Renee come out the office. She carefully counted exact change into the little girl's hand.

"Thank you, Miss Renee," Brittany said and gave her a shy smile.

"You're welcome," she said and watched them for a few seconds, waved, then closed the door.

"Waving goodbye to the girls?" he asked when she walked into the library.

"No. I waved to their mother. She was waiting for them on the sidewalk."

This place was more like Mayberry than he thought. When he was growing up, he didn't see his mother until she came home from work and there was no extra money for activities that required selling candy.

"Did you buy three boxes of candy so Brittany could meet her goal?"

She looked at him in surprise. "How did you know?"

"I heard Brandy telling her that she was done. That was really nice."

"It was no problem. They're sweet little girls and I can give the candy to Aunt Gert and her friends."

"You're a generous woman, so why marry Marc? You did say you didn't love him," he restated, making sure that he hadn't misunderstood her. He'd bet his badge that she wasn't the kind of woman who married a man for his money. He'd met that type when he hung out with his friend, Will Johnson, and Renee Foster was the total opposite type.

"No. I didn't love Marc. We didn't marry for love."

Part of him, the part buried deep inside him, gave a primal scream of joy. She hadn't loved his brother and that knowledge filled him with a desire to claim her as his own. He quickly pushed the feeling aside. He knew better. He'd been burned more than once by wanting and never having. He frowned. "So why did you marry him?"

She looked down at the books on the table. "I

wanted to have a family of my own and I thought he would learn to care for me." She shook her head. "I should have known better."

He wanted to take away her pain and tell her that everything would be all right. But he couldn't. His brother had lied enough to her.

"It doesn't matter now," she continued. "All that matters is finding the necklace."

He nodded. The sooner they found the necklace, the sooner he could forget the pain and hurt he'd seen in her eyes. The sooner he could bury the longing he felt when he was around her. He picked up the necklace receipt. "We'll start here."

Chapter 5

"What's wrong with what I have on?" Renee stood in the middle of her office, obviously not pleased.

Chris looked at the baggy, shapeless black dress, black tights and butt-ugly shoes Renee wore. He'd seen better looking shoes on the homeless. He'd asked her to dress like a grieving widow for the trip to the jewelry store. He wanted the sight of Renee to make the person at the store feel sorry for her. He'd used the sympathy card a few times in his career to get information from a reluctant employer in the past and it was worth a try now.

While she'd gone upstairs to change clothes, he'd made quick work of exploring the main level of the house, searching for something that would explain her knowledge of computers. It had given him something to think about, other than her taking off her clothes upstairs.

He tilted his head to the side. "If you walk in the store wearing that, the staff will expect you to ask for a handout." He should know. He and Marc had worn donated clothes several sizes too big while growing up. Today, they would have been in fashion, but then the way they dressed advertised their poverty. Too many store employees to count had followed them around. To them, poverty was synonymous with shoplifting and Marc had proven them correct.

She looked down at herself and brushed her hands along the sides of the dress. "No way. I wear this to work all the time."

Chris raised his brows. Why did she wear clothes at least a size too big? "Do you have something more tailored in black?"

She wrinkled her brow. "I've got a black suit." Her voice was uncertain.

"Let's see it." He put his hands in his pockets.

"I don't think what I look like is going to make a difference one way or the other. I just want to know if they have Aunt Gert's necklace."

"You haven't reported the necklace as stolen. Legally the store doesn't have to answer any of our questions. We need to give them a reason to want to tell us what we want to know. Changing clothes should be a small price to pay if the store leads us to the necklace."

She straightened her shoulders then nodded. "You're right. I'll be right back."

Chris watched her leave the room. The dress hung like a black tent around her frame, making her look smaller than she was. He hoped she didn't question everything that he suggested otherwise it was going to be a very long two weeks. Moments later, he turned at the quiet sound of her footsteps on the stairs and felt a pull of desire so strong he nearly groaned.

She stood in the doorway looking sexy, feminine and vulnerable. The black suit hugged every inch of her curves. Her breasts looked full and lush. Who knew her baggy clothes covered a small waist and full hips that had him thinking of him, her and a bed. She pulled on the jacket as if pulling it would hide the curvy body within. The skirt showed off long legs that were nice. Very nice. She looked up and met his gaze and for the first time he did nothing to hide his desire.

Her eyes widened in surprise and confusion before she looked down. "Is this what you were talking about?"

"Absolutely. You look beautiful."

She frowned and shifted her weight from one foot to the other before she caught herself and stood perfectly still. "Thank you."

He could tell that she was uncomfortable and he

wondered why a simple compliment would cause that kind of reaction. "Are you ready to go?"

"I just need to get my purse."

The twenty-minute drive to H. Morgan and Sons Jewelers was filled mostly with silence. Renee didn't say much other than to give him directions. The jewelry store was located in a small strip mall with a Tuscan facade in an upscale neighborhood. He drove past the valet and parked in an empty spot in the postage-size parking lot. He put the car in Park and turned to her. "Okay, here's the plan. I want you to look like you're struggling to put on a brave face in your grief. If you're asked questions, try to make your voice waver. Do you think you can do that?"

She pressed her lips together and frowned. "I think I can."

"Good. If we're lucky, we'll get the information today. If we don't, don't worry about it. I'll keep coming back until I get it. Okay?"

She nodded.

He looked into her somber brown eyes and saw a hint of uneasiness, but an even greater amount of determination and strength. He nodded, then opened his door and walked around the car. Before he could reach the passenger side, Renee opened her door and stepped out. He brushed aside his annoyance and walked beside her. The hot Alabama sun beamed down on them. He reached for the store's door seconds ahead of her. He waited until she looked at him. "Renee, I open doors for women. Always."

She stepped back. "Oh, well. All right then."

He opened the door and gestured her inside.

The interior of the store had an air of old-world elegance. Rich fabric formed the backdrop for elegant pieces of jewelry. Chris scanned the store, noting a young saleswoman helping an older woman who was examining rings at the first counter. A young couple and a salesman were quietly talking near the rear. A security guard stood off to the side at a discreet distance. To the casual observer, the man looked relaxed, but Chris noticed the way his gaze constantly scanned the store. When their gazes met, Chris kept his face blank and nodded his head in greeting. The guard gave him a short nod before continuing his surveillance of the store. They were greeted by an older woman dressed in an immaculate beige suit and pearls. "Welcome. How can I help you today?"

Chris pegged her as the manager. "I hope you can help us Ms.—" he made a show of looking at the discreet name tag on her lapel "—Morgan. We'd like to speak to the manager."

"I'm the owner."

He held out his hand. "I'm Chris Foster and this is my sister-in-law, Renee Foster."

Chris shifted and stepped to the side. From this position, he could watch the door and most of the store. He watched as Renee gave the woman a brief smile and quiet pain shone in her eyes. It wasn't an act. He nearly winced and wished for the nth time that she'd let him do this alone. She'd held herself coolly alone at Flowers Funeral Home during Marc's funeral. Her adamant refusal to deal with him about Marc's estate made him think of her as cold and distant. The emotion he saw on her face clearly proved she wasn't. She should have stayed home. There was nothing he could do to comfort her now other than keep his focus on finding the necklace. He returned his gaze to the owner.

"Nice to meet you both." Ms. Morgan's pleasant expression never wavered.

Chris reached inside his jacket pocket and pulled out the receipt. "My brother, Marc, died in April and we found this receipt in some of his papers. This might be the necklace he bought to give Renee for her birthday. We can't find the necklace any-where." He paused, maintaining eye contact with the older woman, searching for any sign of sym-pathy.

He didn't see any.

"We know he bought several pieces of jewelry from your store and we'd like to know what the necklace looked like. If we can't find it, Renee would like to buy a replacement."

The older woman looked from him to Renee. Her expression remained politely friendly.

"I'm sorry for your loss," she said and he could tell she truly meant it.

"Thank you," he said. "It would be a big help if you could tell us about this piece."

She took the receipt, looked at it and returned it. "How do I know you are who you say you are?"

"Here's my ID." He held it out for her.

She looked at it for a long time. "I'm going to call and verify the information."

"That's fine," he said and gave her a business card. "You can call the main number and they can give you verification."

She went to one of the counters and made the call. A few minutes later she returned.

"May I have the…" She stopped when a discreet melody signaled the arrival of another customer.

Chris looked toward the door. The couple standing just inside the store dressed the part of upper middle-class man and woman. The woman wore a lightweight minidress with a matching long jacket that was almost as long as the dress. The heels on her sandals were so high he wondered how she managed to walk. She carried a purse the size of his overnight bag and her sunglasses covered her slightly tanned face. The guy wore a gray suit and blue shirt unbuttoned at the collar. He looked like he'd left his high-level job, ditched his tie and brought his lady to buy something expensive. There wasn't anything about them that should have made the hair on the back of his neck stand on end, but it did.

He felt an icy beat of tension spread around him

and kept his eye on them, carefully moving his hand toward his weapon. The woman took off her sunglasses and moved her shoulder to let one of the straps of the purse drop to the side. She turned slightly, pulled open her purse, slipping the sunglasses inside. He had the weapon in his hand and reached for Renee when he saw the woman pull a gun from the bag.

She'd shot the guard without uttering a word. He heard the sound of screams and he'd squeezed off a single round. He didn't watch her fall, but trained his weapon on the other half of the couple. The man's face turned chalk-white as Chris stood there with his arms out in front of him, the gun grasped between his hands pointed at him.

"FBI. Put it down," he said, watching the man's eyes widen and blink. Breathing hard, the guy kept his gaze steady as he stepped to the side toward the woman. The barrel of the gun never wavered and stayed on him.

"Situation," the man said with a slightly Slavic accent.

Chris didn't know what the hell the man was talking about. "Put your weapon down," he bit out. He had no way of knowing what was going on in the rest of the store. He kept his focus on the man in front of him and hoped like hell everyone was down on the floor, out of the line of fire. The sound of whimpers and crying filled the store.

The man took another step and stood beside the

woman lying on the floor, blood now covering the front of her dress.

"Situation." His voice was louder this time, never taking his eyes off Chris.

The tingly beep of what sounded like an alarm from a watch or cell phone came from the woman's purse. He saw the man's green eyes flash with icy rage then go carefully blank. Chris dived to the side and squeezed the trigger twice. He vaguely registered the sound of glass exploding to his right and watched as the man fell back before his shoulder hit the hard floor. He rolled, keeping his gun trained toward the man. Seconds later, he got to his feet and moved carefully toward the front of the store. Blood seeped from two holes in the man's chest. He stepped over the man's gun that lay a few feet away. The man's chest raised and lowered and he could hear the ragged sound of his breathing. The woman remained motionless, crumpled on the floor beneath a pool of blood. He walked to the security guard and kneeled on the floor beside him. Chris pressed fingers to the man's neck and was glad to feel a faint pulse.

He stood, then turned his gaze toward the rear of the store. Renee lay on the floor. Her face was pale and she watched him. He saw the fear and terror in her wide brown eyes. He'd had no choice but to shoot them. Would she look at him with disgust now that she'd seen firsthand that he could kill? He saw no condemnation in her expression and felt a wave of relief. Why did he care what she thought?

He watched her take a shaky breath, then place a small white object on the floor beside her and rise to her feet. He tightened his jaw against the urge to go and comfort her. Curious, he looked closely at the container.

Mace. He jerked his gaze back to her and knew she would have fought back if given a chance. A part of him admired her bravery even as he blocked out the terrifying thought of her attempting to use Mace against armed robbers. He looked away, pushed aside his feelings and scanned the room. Ms. Morgan lay on the floor beside Renee with her hands covering her face and the young couple lay huddled on the floor in the back holding hands. The woman's sobs made her shoulders shake.

"Is anyone hurt?" His voice was sharp. He saw the salesman rise hesitantly from behind the counter. "I'm fine," the man said, looking around the room. "Mom," he yelled when he saw Ms. Morgan on the floor. Chris watched the man run to the woman. The young man looked at his mother, then said, "We're…" His voice sounded weak and a little shaky. He cleared his throat and repeated. "We're okay."

The saleswoman got to her feet and leaned against the counter. "I'm good," she said.

Chris nodded and lowered his gun. "Did anybody sound the alarm?"

"I did," the other saleswoman said, leaning against the counter as if it were the only thing holding her upright.

Renee walked toward him. He saw fear struggle with worry. "Are you all right?" Her voice was soft and she gripped the straps of her purse in her hand.

Chris felt something shift inside him. "I'm fine." He looked at the three people who lay bleeding on the floor and returned his gaze to her.

Her lips tightened and she came toward him.

He shook his head. "No. Stay there." He didn't want her to see the violence up close.

She ignored him. When she stood in front of him, she reached inside her purse and pulled out a tissue then pressed it to his cheek. "You're bleeding," she said.

He looked on the floor where he'd been standing when he shot the man. Shattered glass from the display case lay on the floor. A piece of it must have cut him.

With his free hand, he reached up and grasped her wrist and felt her tremble. Gently he pulled her hand and the blood-smeared tissue away from his face. Suddenly he felt the sting of pain on his cheek and knew he'd feel more pain once the adrenaline wore off. But it was the warmth of her touch that stayed with him and made him feel emotions he didn't want to examine. "I'm fine," he said and squeezed her hand.

She stared into his eyes for a long moment

before nodding her head. She pulled her hand away and he released her, strangely reluctant to let her go. He watched her straighten her shoulders and look at the man holding a now-crying Ms. Morgan. She turned as if to look toward the victims. "Don't," he said and moved to block her view.

She said nothing, but looked at him, then turned so she had her back to the victims and walked toward Ms. Morgan. He watched her reach for her purse before kneeling on the other side of the older woman who was now sitting up, leaning against the man. Renee opened her purse and pressed another tissue in the woman's hand.

Chris unclipped his cell phone and began dialing. The local cops should be here soon but they needed to get multiple ambulances here. As he listened to the phone ring, he studied Renee and wondered what other surprises lay beneath her quiet demeanor. He wondered if he could continue to resist a woman he found absolutely fascinating.

Twenty minutes later, Renee shifted in a hard plastic chair that had been positioned in front of one of the glass display cases, watching the buzz of activity. She didn't know how Chris had known she was considering sitting on the floor. Her knees had begun to feel about as stable as warm Jell-O and she was afraid she'd end up sprawled on the carpet in an unsightly heap if they gave out. Somehow, he'd known how she was feeling and had the salesman get a chair for her and the rest of the women.

She was shaken, as Aunt Gert liked to say, but shaken didn't begin to cover how she felt. Watching three people get shot was catching up with her, but she refused to curl up in a fetal position and cry like she wanted. Crying would wait until she was at home alone. Like always.

Mountain View police officers seemed to swarm the store. She'd already spoken to one of the policemen and told him her version of what had happened. Chris had remained close during the whole process. For that, she was grateful. She hated to admit it, but she didn't like dealing with the police. It brought back memories she wanted to keep buried.

She moved her gaze from a woman taking pictures of the wall and looked at Chris, who was flanked by two officers. He looked calm, controlled and totally comfortable in what to her seemed like chaos. She supposed he was comfortable. He worked for the FBI. She was anything but comfortable and it was getting harder for her to hold it together as time went on.

She was so glad Chris had been here. She kept thinking about what could have happened. Who knew what the robbers had planned to do? They could have killed everyone if Chris hadn't been there. He'd reacted so quickly and pushed her out of harm's way before she'd even fully understood what was happening. He'd put his life on the line to protect all of them with no hesitation. At that moment, she knew she'd made the right decision when she'd asked for his help. Today, he'd shown her that she could trust him with her life.

Her hands began to shake and they felt cold. She rubbed them on her skirt to warm them. She wanted to go home. She wanted to sit in her library and look at her books and enjoy the peace and quiet and forget she ever stepped foot inside this store.

Weariness settled on her like a heavy blanket. She leaned back in the chair and wished for the day to end. Chris turned and looked at her. It was as if he had some sort of radar when it came to her. He said something to one of the officers and walked toward her looking as polished as if he'd just started his day. When he reached her chair, he leaned down, his golden-brown eyes level with her own.

"We can leave now," he said, his voice deep and calm.

She put the strap of her purse on her arm and stood. He walked at her side, guiding her through the maze of law enforcement officers toward the front of the store. She shuddered when she saw the dark stains of blood on the carpet. For one brief moment, she went back in time and heard the sound of gunfire and saw the guard falling, flying back like he'd been punched with a giant fist.

She felt Chris put his arm around her and shift

to block her view of the bloody floor. She stared at the bright white cotton of his dress shirt.

"It's over, Renee." He gave her shoulders a squeeze and lifted her chin.

She looked at his face and into eyes that were becoming more familiar. "It's over," he said.

His quiet strength surrounded her, supporting her just as his arms supported her now.

"I want to go home," she said then bit her lip to stop the trembling.

He led her out of the store and for once she was grateful for the hot summer sun.

Renee tried to focus on gently rolling hills that surrounded Mountain View, but in her mind, she saw the woman shooting the guard. That scene played over and over in her head like a bad movie stuck on repeat. Her chest felt tight and her breathing was short, shallow and way too fast. She was going to have to calm down or else she was going to lose it. Big-time. She was too far gone to close her eyes and meditate. She was scared. Scared to experience again the total helplessness and stunned disbelief she'd felt in the store. Afraid to think about what would have happened if Chris hadn't been in the store with her.

No, she said to herself, *I'm not going to lose it.* She was fine. What she needed was something to do. Anything to take her mind off what she'd witnessed today. Renee looked down at her purse on the seat beside her and yanked it open, nearly spilling its contents onto the floor. She pulled out her PDA. It contained all her appointments and to-do list. She opened her to-do list. Buy groceries was first on the list. She quickly opened a blank screen and began writing. It didn't matter that she had a grocery list on her laptop at home. What mattered now was having something to do because thinking about anything other than what was in the aisles of Bruno's grocery store was more than she could handle.

Chris divided his attention between the winding road leading back to Renee's house and Renee. It sounded as if she were sending messages in Morse code on her PDA and he was pretty sure she didn't realize she was tapping her foot. The bad part was she was tapping it so fast it was making him feel tired.

He cursed silently. He wanted a shower, a cold beer and a good baseball game playing on the television, but he knew he wouldn't get any of them today. He couldn't let her face what was coming alone.

She had all the signs of someone getting ready to crash and crash hard. He knew the signs because he'd been where she was right now. The hell of it was it was going to get worse and she didn't even know it was coming.

Renee looked up when the car came to a stop. They were parked in front of her house and she was so glad to be home. She stuffed her PDA back into her purse and reached for the handle on the door to get out. She was pulled back against the seat by the seat belt. Smooth, Renee. Real smooth, she thought as she fumbled with the release mechanism. She frowned when the buckle slipped from her hands for the second time. Her hands were shaking so hard that she couldn't release the seat belt. Renee pressed her lips together in concentration and tried again and missed again.

Chris reached across and disengaged her seat belt. His hands looked hard, strong and steady. Thankful and a little embarrassed, she moved the belt out of her way and got out. She swung the strap of the purse over her shoulder and walked toward her house. She moved quickly up the walkway then climbed the stairs to the porch. She needed to get Chris inside the house and on his way because she didn't know how long she could hold it together.

She opened her purse and took her keys out of the zippered pocket before promptly dropping them on the porch. Feeling heat rush to her cheeks, she bent down to get them. It took major effort to pick them up with her hand shaking so much and she nearly dropped them again. When she stood, she gave him a small, embarrassed smile. With unsteady hands, she separated the key to the front door and tried to insert it into the lock. The more she tried the more her hands shook. She blinked back the tears that were threatening to fall. She wasn't going to cry. She wasn't.

She gripped the key and moved it toward the lock once more, then she felt the warmth and strength of Chris's hand covering her own. Slowly, gently, he steadied her hand and she put the key in the lock and opened the door.

She wanted to go inside and shut him out. She didn't want to face him, to see pity in his expression. She'd seen enough of that when she was in school. But she couldn't ignore him and she wasn't a coward. She stepped inside and closed the door. When she turned to face him, she didn't see pity. She saw strength, compassion and a world of understanding. He understood her, not the image she presented to other people, but her. For the first time, she realized that this man saw the real woman and he accepted who she was. She could just be.

The tears she'd been fighting to suppress welled in her eyes before streaming down her cheeks. Chris moved forward, wrapping his arms around her, and held her while she cried.

Chapter 6

Chris held her and continued to hold her long after the hard, gut-wrenching sobs gave way to silent tears. It was damn hard listening to her cry. He wanted to comfort her, to wipe away the images he was sure would haunt her tonight. But he knew he could no more prevent her from suffering than he could make his mother stay in one place when he was a boy. So, he held her and hoped it was enough.

She was tougher than she looked. She hadn't cried out when the first shots were fired like one of the other women in the store. His training and experience had prepared him for all kinds of scenarios, but even those with training sometimes fell apart when the bullets flying were real and coming toward you. Renee had held it together before, during and after the robbery, which made what he'd had to do a lot easier. For her sake, he hoped both the suspects survived, but he'd deal with it if they didn't. He'd had to deal with killing a suspect as a cop in California. He had fellow cops and the departmental shrink to help. He hoped Renee had someone she could turn to for help.

He looked down and rubbed her back. Holding her felt…right. In the past, he'd always felt awkward giving comfort to a woman, but comforting her was as natural as breathing. She was quieter now and the shudders, which had racked her body, had been reduced to the occasional shiver. The steady ticktock of the grandfather clock filled the silence and he felt her shift. Reluctantly he loosened his embrace.

She wiped the tears from her cheeks and when she looked up at him with her chocolate-brown eyes, he wanted to take her in his arms again.

"I…" She cleared her throat. "Thank you—" her voice was deeper "—for everything."

He didn't know why she was thanking him. He'd been doing his job. What he'd been trained to do, but she didn't want nor did she need to hear that. "You're welcome," he said. She looked tired and not quite steady on her feet.

"I know we agreed to work more today, but I

can't do it. Not after—" She stopped. "Do you think they'll let us know how the guard is doing?"

"I'll see what I can find out." Technically the hospital would only release the bare amount of information about a patient to non–family members.

He'd go to the hospital himself to learn the man's condition if it would make her life a little easier. She looked as if she was remaining upright by sheer will. "Is there anyone you want to call? You shouldn't to be alone tonight."

She shook her head. "No. Aunt Gert won't be back from Biloxi for a few days. I'll be okay. I'm just tired."

There was no way in hell he was going to leave her alone. He remembered all too well the nights he'd been haunted by hellish nightmares. His friend Will had shown up at his apartment with a one-hundred-and-five-dollar bottle of Scotch and pizza. He didn't remember eating much, but the Scotch had gone down warm and smooth when he'd awakened in a cold sweat. Reliving the moments when he wasn't sure if he'd be fast enough to squeeze the trigger of his gun before an enraged ex-husband made good on his promise to kill his ex-wife and children.

He would have to stay with her. "I need to go through Marc's stuff again. Why don't I hang out down in the office down here. I can let myself out when I leave."

"I don't…"

He spoke over her obvious reluctance. "And I

need a secure Internet connection to check on the Florida driver's license since we didn't get information from the jewelry store." It was a lie. He could get that information without using her network, but it was a good excuse to stay with her tonight.

She frowned, looking uncertain. "All right, but let me know when you leave so I can lock the dead bolt."

"I can lock it when I leave."

"How? You don't have a key."

He smiled. "I don't need a key to lock it." He watched her frown deepen and he could all but hear her thinking. "Trust me, Renee. When I leave, your house will be locked up tight."

For a few seconds, she just looked at him, then the frown disappeared. "I trust you. Stay as long as you need to and you're welcome to whatever's in the kitchen."

"Thanks. See you tomorrow." He moved slowly toward the office all the while listening to her soft footsteps along the hardwood floor and up the stairs. When she was out of sight, he moved silently to the stairway. She moved as if the weight of the world was on her shoulders and he wanted to go up the stairs and let her know that she wouldn't have to deal with this alone.

That would go over really well. She didn't want me in her house in the first place.

She turned left and seconds later he heard the sound of a door closing. He went to the library, which was directly below the room she'd entered. He was guessing it was the master bedroom and he heard two soft thuds coming from above. Seconds passed and when he didn't hear anything more, he walked across the hall to the office and picked up the laptop and briefcase that he'd left on the desk and came back to the library. He grimaced at the two chairs covered in frills sitting near the windows and went to the overstuffed leather chair.

He opened his laptop and slid a thin card into place. In no time, he began going through a series of passwords and identification verifications that would get him on a secured network. Minutes later, he was up and running without using her Internet connection. He didn't know how the card worked and didn't care. He checked his e-mail to see if someone from the DMV had responded to his request. No one had, which wasn't unexpected.

He heard a muffled cough and turned in the chair and looked up. There was an ornate white grate on the wall about a foot down from the ceiling. Good, he thought, he could hear her upstairs. He returned his attention to his laptop and went through the messages in his in-box. He was glad to see Will's e-mail address and he read the message. Give me a call.

Chris got out his cell phone.

"Johnson."

"It's Chris."

"Damn, man. We can't let you go anywhere.

What's this I hear about you taking out two people in a jewelry store?"

"Word travels fast."

"Yeah. I heard about it on CNN. They don't have your name yet. So fill me in."

Chris told him what happened in the store. It didn't surprise him that Will had heard about the shooting. Despite his laid-back demeanor, Will was well connected. They'd never discussed who he or his wealthy, influential family members knew, but rumor was Will could get the ear of just about any high-level official in law enforcement on a national level and that he even had the ear of the president.

"You know this is just going to make Chief more determined then ever to get you back."

Chief was his old boss in the police force. He had tried his best to talk him out of going to the bureau. He was a cop's cop and considered the feds a necessary and unpleasant evil. Chief couldn't understand why he'd wanted to leave when he was about to be promoted. Chris had tried to explain that this decision had nothing to do with the job. He'd made up his mind years ago when two special agents had met him at the diner where he worked as a waiter at night to pay for college. They'd come to tell him that they found his mother's killer.

His mother and three other members of the cleaning crew had been killed when they arrived to clean an office building adjacent to a jewelry store. The cleaning crew arrived as the thieves were leaving with over two million dollars in jewelry and loose stones. The crew had been gunned down while still inside the van. The agents had gone out of their way to keep him informed even when the case seemed to go cold. He'd never forgotten it.

"I know, but I'm not coming back," Chris said.

"Don't tell me. Tell him, and soon, because he'll be riding my ass to try to get you to change your mind."

"You can handle it."

"Handle it? I don't handle Chief. I stay as far away from him as I can when he's on one of his 'get Chris back to real police work' kicks. That reminds me, my mother wanted me to tell you that you aren't off the hook and she expects you at the house before the end of the year."

The "house" was a mansion located on a private beach in Hawaii and had been featured in *Architectural Digest*.

"I'm going to need a vacation," Chris said. "We went to the jewelry store to find out if Marc took the necklace there. The manager was about to help us when the bullets started flying."

"The whole situation is just crazy. Let me know if I can do anything to help."

"I will. I found a Florida driver's license and another credit card sewn in Marc's clothes."

"How did his wife take it?"

He didn't like hearing Renee called Marc's wife

because he wanted her for himself. "She's strong. She can hold her own."

"I'll bet she'll let you handle finding the necklace by yourself now."

"I wouldn't bet on it. She held it together until she got home."

"Damn," he said with admiration. "Who's staying with her?"

"I am. I told her I needed to look over Marc's stuff again."

"You're just catching hell left and right."

"No kidding. Her great-aunt won't be back in town for a few days." Chris glanced up at the ceiling. All was still quiet upstairs and he hoped it stayed that way for her sake.

"You're staying at her place the whole time?"

"Looks like it—" he glanced over his shoulder to the grate then lowered his voice "—but she doesn't know it."

"I don't hear an echo so she must have furniture in the house. You don't have to sleep on the floor like I did."

"For one night. You need to let that go."

"Get a sofa," Will said.

Chris set the laptop on the floor beside him then stretched his legs out in front of him. This was a familiar discussion. Will believed in comfort, especially at home, and that meant fully furnished. "I don't want a sofa. I'll just have to move it in a few months anyway."

"That's the point."

"I got what I need."

"You use your laptop on a folding tray and use the same tray to eat dinner," he said with disgust.

Will's comment made him think about computers and the number of computers Renee had in her office. "Let me ask you something."

"Yes. I think you should furnish your apartment," he said in a dry tone.

"Go to hell," he said casually. "What do you think about a librarian having at least five computers linked together in her home? She found almost as much information as I did about Marc's finances and movements."

"No kidding." His tone sharpened with interest. "Who did she pay to find all of that?"

"She said she found it herself."

"The librarians that I've had contact with are always looking up books on the computer, not installing computer systems. Where'd she learn to do that and what's with all the computers?"

"She said she studied it in library school. I don't think that's the whole truth. I'm going to find out if she took computer science while she was in college."

"Didn't you tell me she went to college when she was fourteen?"

"Aw, hell. I forgot about that. She could have learned about computers from anywhere."

"And she's smart enough to know where to find the information she didn't know," Will added.

"She told me she had tracking software on her home network and that's how she found one of his credit cards."

"Stay the hell off her network."

"You know it," he said, then paused and held the phone away from his ear. He thought he heard something, but he couldn't be sure, then he heard her. He put the phone back to his ear and said, "I've got to go." Then he hit the end button. He got out of the chair, put the phone in his pocket and walked toward the stairs.

The sound of a low moan came from above. He quickly climbed the stairs. He could make out what she was saying when he reached the second floor. Each word she spoke grew louder and louder.

"No, no, no."

The door to her bedroom was closed. He opened the door and stepped inside.

She lay curled up in the fetal position on top of a four-poster king-size bed. Her jacket was a crumpled pool of black on the floor next to her shoes, which looked like she'd left them exactly where she'd pulled them off.

When he reached the bed, he sat beside her, sinking into the plush mattress. "Renee." He laid his hand on her shoulder. "Wake up, Renee."

She curled tighter into herself as if she were

trying to make herself as small as possible. Her skirt slid up higher on her brown thighs. "No, no."

His heart ached for her. "Renee," he said, his tone sharp enough, he hoped, to break through and awaken her from her personal hell. He tightened his grip on her shoulder.

She jerked awake, her eyes wild with fear and slightly glazed. Then she was in his arms, pressed against him and holding on as if she were never letting go.

"You're safe," he said softly and wrapped his arms around her. "You were dreaming. It was just a dream." He could feel her fear in her shoulders that trembled, hear it still in her whimpers. "You're home."

The soft, sweet scent of her enveloped him as he rocked back and forth, repeating over and over, "You're safe."

"She shot him," she whispered. "She just shot him. It was real."

He rubbed her back. There was nothing he could say that would make the nightmare go away. He knew no matter how much you tried to forget, vivid memories had a way of sneaking up on you in your dreams like a well-planned and executed tactical ambush that left you beaten and defeated.

"I know," he said softly.

She shifted and rubbed her check against his chest. "He was going to try to kill you," she said with strength and certainty in her tone.

He wanted to deny it, but couldn't. She deserved nothing less than the truth from him. He'd asked her to trust him today and she had. She was strong enough to handle the truth. "Yes, he was."

She tightened her arms around him. "You didn't give him the chance. I'm glad you were there with me." She tilted her head and looked up at him. "You're a good person, Chris."

He frowned. "I don't know what to say to you." He hadn't meant to say that to her. Cursing to himself, he watched her closely, hoping his blunt comment didn't hurt her feelings. Rarely was he open and honest with someone. Will was the only person who really knew him, but somehow Renee had slipped beneath his defenses.

He looked away from the tempting sight of her soft, full lips so close to his. She didn't need that kind of attention from him right now. The admiration he saw on her face did nothing to cool the lazy burn of desire beginning to rise inside of him. He wanted her, but he didn't want her to make him into some kind of hero. He was just a man.

She didn't appear to be upset by his remark. In fact, she looked a little less afraid and more like her normal self.

"You don't have to say anything."

He nodded. He should leave. Go back downstairs now that she was okay, but he didn't. "Do you need anything?"

She shook her head. "No. I'm tired, but I don't want to go back to sleep."

"You don't have to sleep now." He knew exactly how she felt; he hadn't wanted to go to sleep, either. He'd tried everything from television to caffeine to keep him awake, but that only worked for a short period of time. Sooner or later the body shut down.

"We never did find out what Marc bought at the store." Her voice was soft and he heard the trace of fear and wariness in her tone.

"We'll figure out something." He'd planned on talking to the manager again. He was sure she would give him the information he wanted.

"I tried to figure something out after the funeral. I tried to hire someone to find the necklace, but everybody I spoke with insisted on telling Aunt Gert the necklace was gone." She frowned and her bottom lip came out. He could imagine her with that same look as a little girl, but she was no little girl. He wanted to sink his teeth into that pouty, sweet lip before letting his tongue trace the line where her lips came together. He looked away and stared down at the floor. He was going to have to get his thoughts under control. *Yeah, right.* He shifted his weight on the bed. He was going to have to get it together before his body betrayed him, but he couldn't let go of her.

"That was the whole point of trying to hire them in the first place," she continued. "When Terrell told me where you worked, I almost asked for your help then."

"Why didn't you?"

"I wasn't sure if I could trust you. You could have been as bad as Marc."

Her honesty was like a punch to the face. "I'm not Marc," he said, not caring if she heard the anger and frustration clearly in his voice. He was tired of paying for something he didn't do.

She nodded. "I knew that when I read the first offer to settle Marc's estate."

He drew back, surprised by her statement. "What? Why didn't you…" He stopped. He knew why she didn't take his offer.

"I didn't want Danielle's company nor did I want any of Alex's money. As Marc's only legal wife, I know I could have fought for those things but I couldn't in good conscience take the business Danielle's brother built. It's her final tie to the brother she loved. And Alex…Alex might look and sound like a piece of fluff, but she's a whole lot smarter than people think." She gave him a somber look. "I think her lawyers scare my lawyer."

He felt his frustration melt away and knew she absolutely trusted him, otherwise she wouldn't have told him any of this before she had the necklace back. "To tell the truth, Alex and her lawyers scare the hell out of me."

She laughed like he intended and she looked more beautiful to him in her wrinkled clothes and her rumpled hair. He knew without a doubt that she would be his.

"I'm more afraid of Danielle. She doesn't take stuff from anybody," she said.

He remembered leaving Renee, Alex and Danielle together while he, Hunter, her friend whom he'd asked to escort Alex to Marc's funeral, and Tristan, Danielle's longtime friend, went to pick up breakfast. When they came back, Alex held her cheek and Renee sat next to her with her arm around the younger woman's shoulder. Danielle looked embarrassed and upset. There was Renee telling them both to behave. Thinking about the two women made him wonder. "Did you ask the others if Marc gave them the necklace?"

"Not specifically. I told them that I was missing a piece of jewelry and asked if Marc had given them diamonds."

He tilted his head, confused. "Why didn't you ask them flat out if they had the necklace?"

"Alex had just told us about her engagement to Hunter. I didn't want to tell her my bad news when it was such a happy time for her."

He shook his head. "Why don't you ask them now. If either of them know anything they would tell you."

"I don't think they know anything. Both of them said the only jewelry Marc gave them was their wedding rings." Her speech had slowed and her eyelids lowered.

"Call them anyway," he said softly. After Alex

told them the diamond in her engagement ring had been replaced with cubic zirconia, Danielle and Renee had their rings appraised when they returned home.

She put her head on his shoulder again and sighed. "Okay, I'll call them in the morning."

He held her, listening as her breathing became slower, steadier. He had no idea how long he sat there, just holding her, but somewhere along the way his desire to give comfort became full-blown desire of another kind. His body reacted to the softness of her breasts pressed against his chest and the warmth of her hands at his back. The rhythm of his breathing changed, growing shorter, faster.

She grew still and he knew she could feel and sense the change in him. He wouldn't be surprised if she drew back and asked him to leave. She tipped her head back and he looked down into her warm brown eyes and saw in them a spark of longing and desire. Just one kiss, he thought as he lowered his head slowly, giving her time to stop him. Then he pressed his mouth to hers. Her lips were soft, warm, sweet. The kind of sweet that had you coming back for more.

Renee moaned with pleasure as Chris used his tongue to trace the seam of her mouth. She parted her lips and felt his tongue tease and beckon. Desire, swift and strong, had her head spinning and her tongue matching the sensual movement of his.

She'd never known that a kiss could give so much hot, wicked pleasure. His hand moved in one slow, lingering stroke down her back, pressing her more tightly against his hard chest. Feeling the strength and power in his broad shoulders, her breasts grew heavy and tight.

He lifted his head and gently nibbled her bottom lip before tilting his head and kissing her again, igniting a need so strong, so compelling, she felt as if every nerve in her body vibrated with lust.

Chris heard his cell phone ringing and groaned in frustration and annoyance. He lifted his head, drawing in an unsteady breath of air. The depth of his desire for her shook him and with the taste of her still on his lips, he wanted more. His phone rang again. Reluctantly he moved out of her embrace and took the phone out of his pocket. He looked at the display before answering.

Minutes later, he closed the phone. During the short conversation, Renee had propped pillows behind her and was now leaning against the cushioned headboard.

Her cheeks were flushed and she played with the hem of her blouse, keeping her gaze on the silky material. He wanted to kiss her, to taste her again, but he could tell she'd pulled back.

"The security guard is out of surgery and expected to recover," he said, watching as her eyes closed and her shoulders relaxed. "The suspects are in critical condition." He put the phone back into his pocket.

"I was worried about the guard. I'm glad he's doing okay."

"Me, too." He was glad she hadn't witnessed such a violent death. "The police think the suspects are responsible for five other robberies in the southeast." They also thought one of them was responsible for killing two people in Kentucky. He'd keep that information to himself.

She looked at him. Her lips were slightly swollen from his kiss, but her eyes were solemn and there was a hint of fear in her gaze. "I'm glad you stopped them. They can't hurt anyone now."

"No. They can't." He thought about the Mace she'd held in her hand. "What were you going to do with the Mace?"

She blinked then frowned. "I don't know. The guy pointed the gun at you and then it was in my hand."

He could see that her energy was beginning to fade. She looked weary and fragile.

"You're tired. Sleep if you can."

"Don't want to sleep in this," she said, her voice growing deeper. She leaned forward and he helped her to her feet. "I'll be right back."

He watched her shuffle to a door that opened into the master bath, and close the door behind her. He put his hands in his pockets. He would wait until she got into bed, then would go back downstairs. She needed sleep. There would be other kisses. He'd make sure of it.

He turned when the door opened a few minutes

later. She'd changed into plain, white cotton pajamas. The sight of her wearing them shouldn't have
aroused him, but it did. Yep, he was going to have
to go back downstairs.

The hem of her top ended just below her waist
and the white material clung to her full breasts. The
drawstring pants neatly hugged her hips. Her body
looked full, lush and tempting. He felt himself hard-
en with desire as she walked toward the bed.

She began pulling back the spread and stumbled.
He caught her shoulders to steady her.

"Here," he said. "Let me do it." He pulled the
spread and sheet down, placed the pillows in a neat
line at the top of the bed. He stepped aside then said,
"In you go."

She climbed in, pulling the sheet to her chest,
and lay on her side.

"Sleep tight," he said softly.

Her lids lowered briefly then she looked at him.
"Will you sit with me? I don't want to be alone."
Her voice began to slur.

So much for going downstairs. He sat on the
mattress. "Yes, I'll stay."

He watched as her lids lowered, her dark lashes
forming black semicircles against her brown skin.
He sat there watching her fall deeper into sleep.

His brother had brought the two of them
together, but he was going to make sure it was him
that she wanted. He'd never met a woman like her
before. She was brave, stubborn and sexy. And she

tried to hide it behind the brainy persona she presented to the world. He watched her and anticipated the day when he would make love to her.

Chapter 7

The next morning, Renee opened her eyes and let her gaze feast upon the most luscious man she'd ever met. She knew Chris would be there like he'd been there during the night to awaken her from the nightmares. He'd held her hand and gone with her to the kitchen to make tea when she'd been too afraid to be by herself. Never once had he made her feel like she was being a burden or a bother.

While she'd been sleeping, he'd moved one of two overstuffed chairs and the matching white ottoman beside the bed so he was always within arm's reach of her. He looked strong and powerful as he lay there sleeping.

He'd kissed her. She stared at his talented lips. His kiss had made her yearn. No other man had made her yearn. She obviously hadn't affected him as much as he affected her because he hadn't said another word about it afterward. She sighed. She wasn't good at kissing. Who could blame her; she could count the number of men she'd kissed on one hand and Marc's kisses didn't last that long.

She had a feeling that if the phone hadn't interrupted them, Chris would have kissed her for a long, long time. She shivered as she remembered the taste of him. *Get a hold of yourself. Put the kiss out of your mind. He has.* She took a deep breath and let her gaze drift down.

He'd removed his tie and unbuttoned the first three buttons on his shirt, revealing part of his muscled, hard chest. Yesterday, she'd found comfort and acceptance in his embrace. And passion.

No, I'm not thinking about that. She watched as his chest rose and fell. She remembered how gentle he'd been yesterday. She'd asked him to stay with her and he had. She'd let down her guard and been totally exposed emotionally. She wondered why she could be herself around him when she was afraid to be herself around family and her close friends, the Smithstones.

Karen Smithstone would have put the blame solely on Renee's parents. As a psychiatrist, she'd explained to her the toxic nature of her relationship with her mom and dad. She'd called her parents two of the most self-absorbed people in the universe. Renee didn't agree with Karen's statement. She knew she was a disappointment to her parents. She was terrified of disappointing Aunt Gert.

She wouldn't disappoint her. With Chris's help, she'd recover the necklace.

Renee moved her gaze from his chest down his arm to the hand that lay on the armrest a few inches from the bed. His fingers were long and lean, and his touch had been her anchor during the night. She wanted to close the few inches of distance between their hands and experience his touch once more, but she wouldn't. She looked at his face and nearly jumped out of her skin when she realized he'd awakened and was looking at her. How did he go from asleep to fully awake without moving or making a single sound?

"Morning," she said, then sat up and tried to smooth down her hair. Last night, she had been too emotionally drained to think about it. She didn't need a mirror to realize that she had to look a mess.

"How are you?" His voice was deeper, richer and sexy. The sound of it made her wonder, would he sound the same the morning after making love?

"I'm okay. I made it through the night." She looked at him, leaning back in the chair with his legs stretched out on the ottoman. When he smiled at her, her pulse begin to race and she thought he looked like every woman's fantasy. "Thank you for staying with me," she said, and was glad when her voice remained even and smooth.

"My pleasure."

She gave him a sad smile. "No, it wasn't. You had to sleep in a chair."

He patted the armrest. "I've slept in worse and it's comfortable for a girly froufrou chair."

She smiled. "I like girly froufrou. Every stick of furniture in here is brand-new and really girly. I told the interior designer that I wanted a fairy princess bedroom for a woman."

He looked around the room then said, "I think she nailed it."

"He."

"Mmm." He rubbed his hand on his chin then rolled his shoulders. "Do you mind if I use your shower? I want to change out of these clothes."

Chris Foster. Shower. Wet and naked. Her mouth became dry as her overactive mind brought the scene into clear focus. Heat rushed to her face as desire filled her. The man could make her hot with words and without even trying.

"Ahhh. Sure, you can use the guest bathroom down the hall." She scrambled off the bed. "I'll get the towels."

Chris watched her race out of the bedroom. It was a good thing because he nearly pulled her off the bed and into his lap at her expression when he'd asked to use her shower. Desire, pure and simple, shone on her face. Soon, he would learn if her body was as expressive as her face. As much as he wanted her, he wouldn't push her. She seemed all right this morning but he would give her a little time.

A few minutes later, she came to the door. "Everything is all set."

He followed her down the hall to a large bathroom. A stack of neatly folded large towels was placed at one end of a double granite vanity with double sinks. She'd placed a bar of soap, new toothbrush still in the box, toothpaste and lotion beside the towels. He wondered if she had guests in her home often. He appreciated her thoughtfulness. "I'm going to the car to get my suitcase."

He made the trip to the car, got his suitcase and was back inside within minutes. Locking the front door, he went upstairs. He heard water running when he walked past her closed bedroom door. His body became hard as he imaged her standing naked beneath a warm stream of water showering down on her skin.

He walked to the extra bathroom with long strides. He needed a cold shower and he needed it now.

Showered and dressed, Chris followed the smell of coffee to the kitchen. Renee held a big wooden spoon and stirred something in a large white bowl. She stood with her back to him and he studied her.

She wore white pants and a long, black-and-white-striped shirt. Her hair was pulled into a thick ponytail.

He watched her take the spoon out of the bowl then scoop out a handful of flour from an open plastic bin. She shook her hand back and forth, spreading the flour over the countertop. Her movements were smooth and practiced like she'd performed the act many times in the past. She used the spoon to scrape the sticky, white blob from the bowl onto the countertop.

"What's that?" He walked to the island where there was a full pot of coffee, two cups and spoons, sugar and a small black-and-white container shaped in the form of a smiling cow.

She turned around and he blinked. She wore an apron—not the kind he'd seen chefs wear but the kind he'd seen June Cleaver wear on the *Leave it to Beaver* television show. The apron was white with a large cake sewn on the pocket and smaller cakes lining the ruffled bottom. He wouldn't have thought that she would wear something that…retro.

"Biscuit dough," she said, then floured her hands and pinched off a part of the dough and began rolling it in her hands. "Breakfast will be ready soon."

"Thanks." He saw a carton of eggs beside the stovetop. Biscuits and eggs might be enough for her to have for breakfast, but he hadn't eaten dinner last night and he was starving. On the counter beside the refrigerator sat a large cookie jar in the form of a smiling, pink pig wearing a white chef's hat and apron. She had a thing for smiling farm animals. He hoped the jar had the same cookies she'd given him yesterday.

"Do you mind if I use your phone to call the hotel?" He nodded to the cordless phone. "I need find out if they still have a room available." He wouldn't use the room tonight because he planned to stay here again. He didn't want her to be alone if she had nightmares again tonight.

"You don't have to stay at a hotel. You can stay here in the house or in the guest suite over the garage. That way we could work longer and find the necklace faster." She finished speaking in a rush of words.

He poured coffee into a cup and took a sip. She was offering him the perfect out. Now he wouldn't have to think of a reason to stay. "That'll work." He took another sip. "I spoke to Ms. Morgan from the jewelry store this morning. The necklace Marc bought from them was a string of diamonds from the 1940s. She called all of the employees and none of them have seen your great-aunt's necklace."

She nodded and turned back to the biscuits. "I'm going to call Alex and Danielle after breakfast. I wonder what he's done with that necklace? I don't have it, and I've even checked the cabinet over the refrigerator."

Hunter had discovered Marc's fake divorce

papers and the deed to the yacht in Alex's cabinets above her refrigerator.

"I don't know," Chris said. He could think of several things his brother could have done with the necklace, but sharing that information would only upset her.

"Marc married three women, so there's no telling how many girlfriends he had. He could have given the necklace to one of his girlfriends." She looked at him with horror. "What if he gave Aunt Gert's necklace to another woman?"

"Hey, calm down. Don't think the worst," he said.

"How can I not? You know, I thought I was lucky to have married Marc. Most men don't even consider dating someone like me, but Marc did."

"What do you mean someone like you?"

She shrugged her shoulders. "People like me end up alone, living with multiple cats."

"What are you talking about? You don't have a cat and librarians get married."

She took the pan, which was now covered with biscuits, to the oven. The scent of bacon poured into the room when she opened the oven door. Inside was another pan filled with what looked like a pound of bacon. His mouth began to water. Breakfast was beginning to look a whole lot better. "It's not about being a librarian. It's me. I've been on less than ten dates in my life. I'm not date material."

"That's a bunch of bull. Did Marc tell you that?"

"No. My mother told me," she replied casually as she pulled out the pan of bacon and moved it to another drawer below the oven.

Her mother. He shook his head. He'd seen first-hand the way some parents treated their children when he was a policeman in California. Abuse crossed all racial and economic boundaries. "Your mother is wrong."

"The numbers don't lie."

"If that were true, then financial fraud wouldn't exist."

She waved her hand as if to push his comment aside. "All I'm saying is marrying Marc seemed like the right thing to do at the time. He was my one shot at having a family of my own."

He studied her face. She was serious. Her mother and Marc had done a good job of messing with her head and making her think no one wanted her. She wanted a family and a home. He didn't want either.

When he was a boy he'd wanted to have that kind of life, but he was too jaded to believe anything was permanent. He couldn't give her what she wanted, but he could show her that she was sexy. A woman *this* man wanted to get to know on a very intimate level.

The telephone rang, sending her to the end of the counter. He took another sip of coffee.

She looked at the number on the screen and smiled. "Good morning, Aunt Gert." She moved to the stovetop and lifted the top off a pot.

A few minutes later, he tuned out the conversation. It was girl talk. That's what he called it when he heard women use a lot of words to say something that could have been said in two. He sat down on one of the bar stools and watched her. She was very much in her element in the kitchen. She moved from the stove to a cabinet and began setting the small table in the corner. Her movements were smooth and graceful, but her clothes were wrong. Her pants were baggy and the black-and-white horizontal striped shirt hung on her shoulders like a sack. The apron she wore showed off her small waist. With the exception of the suit she wore yesterday, all of the clothes he'd seen her wear were too big. Instead of her mother telling her she wasn't date material, the woman should have taught her how to dress better.

When the tone of her voice changed, he began listening to the conversation.

"Oh, you called last night." She opened a drawer then closed it without removing a single thing. "I fell asleep early last night."

He watched as her eyes widened and she leaned her hip against the counter.

"You're coming back today? Why? I thought you were having fun?"

He listened as she used sounds, not words, to hold up her end of the conversation, throwing in the occasional "oh" and "really."

"Okay, see you in a few hours. Yes, I'll

remember to bring it." She ended the call and put the phone on its charger. "Aunt Gert wants to meet you." She sounded distracted.

"Is that a problem?"

"No. No. Just don't tell her about the necklace and…" She folded her arms. "I haven't told her about Alex and Danielle and I'd appreciate it if you didn't, either."

"I can do that," he said softly. "I'll talk to her about Marc and I'll let you make the decision to inform her or not about them."

"If I had my way, she'll never know about any of this." She opened the door to the oven and pulled out a pan of golden-brown biscuits. "Breakfast is ready."

He looked forward to meeting her great-aunt. Maybe then he'd understand why Renee was so afraid to tell her about the necklace. Thirty minutes later, he put the last of the dirty dishes into the dishwasher. He'd insisted on doing the dishes. Even after washing the pans by hand, he thought it was worth it. Renee made the best biscuits he'd ever tasted. In fact, everything she'd cooked was delicious—even the grits. The first time he'd tried grits, he thought they had the consistency and flavor of old paste.

"So, what's for lunch?" He closed the dishwasher.

She stopped wiping down the counter and stared at him. "You can't possibly be hungry."

"I'm not, but I want something to look forward to this afternoon. You're a great cook."

"Thank you. Aunt Gert taught me to cook. Now, she's a great cook."

"Your mother didn't teach you?"

She laughed. "My mother doesn't cook. Besides, I wasn't with them long enough to learn to cook. I went to boarding school when I was six."

"Your parents sent you to boarding school for the first grade?" From Will, he'd learned that some wealthy parents shipped their children to boarding schools. While Renee's parents were well-off, they were by no means rich.

She tilted her head and narrowed her eyes. "Yes, and it's not that uncommon to go to school away from home."

Touchy, he thought. "I've never heard of anyone going that young. It's different."

She frowned at him. "Different. Yes, I'm very different." She turned and walked out of the kitchen.

Very touchy. He followed her into the office. She marched to the desk she'd used yesterday and opened her laptop. Her expression was tight.

"Look, I was making conversation. I wasn't trying to make you mad, so forget I asked."

"Fine," she replied with a sharp tone.

He went to the desk and removed the papers he'd been working on last night from his briefcase. *Why was she so angry?* He didn't think his question was out of line. It was strange to send a first-grader to boarding school, and talking about it obviously bothered her. Since she didn't want to talk about her education, he would talk about the necklace and Marc.

"You should call Alex and Danielle now. Marc might have said something to them about the necklace."

She picked up the phone from the desk and began dialing. He listened as she left messages for each of them. When she'd finished, she resumed typing on her laptop and said not a word to him.

Okay. She was ignoring him. He got the message loud and clear and he'd let it go for now.

He looked at the list of airline flights Marc had taken over the past six months. He'd done a lot of traveling, going from the East Coast to the West Coast a few times a month. His job and three wives had kept him busy.

Chris wondered about Marc's job. Marc had worked for Tyche International for four years, which was a year longer than his fake marriage to his first wife, Danielle.

The last time he'd spoken with Marc was two years ago. Marc had called him out of the blue. He'd wanted them to meet at one of the trendy restaurants in Los Angeles for dinner. He hadn't wanted to go. Working twelve- to sixteen-hour days for two months trying to track down the group who'd stolen millions of dollars' worth of diamonds in L.A.'s diamond district had left him bone-tired and frustrated.

When Marc asked him to be the executor of his estate because he trusted him to take care of his family, he agreed to meet Marc. His brother knew which buttons to push. Their father had died weeks before he was to marry their mother and without a will. Without his father's military benefits, she had little money to support herself, Marc and him.

Once Marc had given him a preliminary copy of his will, which already named him as the executor, he and Marc had little to talk about to each other.

They might as well have been strangers. Marc talked about his job, the deals he'd made and the places he'd traveled. Looking back, Chris realized his brother had said very little about his wife that night. Make that wives—Marc had been "married" to both Danielle and Renee at the time. Marc could have said something to one of his coworkers. He wondered if one of them knew about Marc's many wives?

He swiveled around in the chair to face Renee. She was frowning at the screen, typing fast and hard. Her body language shouted "Leave me the hell alone." Although, now that he thought about it, he realized she hadn't said a single curse word since he'd met her. He raised his brows in surprise when he saw her frown deepen and her shoulders hunch forward.

How long, he wondered, would she stare at the computer, pretending he wasn't in the room? From the stubborn look on her face, he'd bet a very long time.

He'd love to pit his skills in persuasion against

her stubborn will. She'd proven how stubborn she could be by refusing to settle Marc's estate and refusing to meet with him after the funeral. She'd won those battles, but he was certain she wouldn't win when she had to go against him in person. He thought about the kiss they'd shared and was sure that with time, he could turn her anger into passion. But time was the one thing they couldn't waste if they were going to find the necklace.

"Giving me the silent treatment isn't going to help us find the necklace."

He could see the internal war on her face. Her frown remained firmly in place. Oh, yeah, she was still mad, but he also saw the speculation in her eyes as she weighed her choices. Talk or ignore him? He had no doubt that she'd talk.

She hadn't handled that well. She'd been rude to him and having been too many times on the receiving end of rude behavior, she didn't like being rude to others. Still, she did *not* want to talk to him. He hadn't pushed her personal hot button. He'd hit it with a sledgehammer.

As a child, she'd had no control over her education. She went to school where her parents told her to go. Her parents had always made it seem as if they were giving up so much to send her to school, when in fact, they hadn't given up a thing. The only time they really paid attention to her was when her

grades were in. They hadn't cared that she was
lonely or scared. No matter how much she told
them that she loved them and wanted to live with
them, they'd brought her back to school and left her.
Years later, Renee had begged to live with Aunt
Gert, but she'd learned that it was useless to ask.
Her parents wouldn't consider it.

Her education wasn't something she liked to
discuss. When people learned that she'd never
attended first through fifth grades, they looked at
her as if she was some kind of a freak.

That's what bothered her. Chris had been so sweet
and kind with her last night, she didn't want to see
pity or disdain on his face when he looked at her.

"I'm sorry," she said softly. "I shouldn't have
snapped at you. It's just that I'm really sensitive
about my education."

"I noticed, and we don't have to discuss it if it
bothers you."

"I might as well tell you about it. It's probably
in the background check you ran on me."

"What makes you think I ran a background
check on you?" His tone was neutral. He had run a
check on her and the other wives.

"I had you investigated, so I would think you
would have done a background check on all three
of Marc's wives. Any one of us had reason to hurt
or maybe kill him if we'd learned what he'd done
to us. Just so you know, I had nothing to do with
his death."

"I know. You were working at the university library when Marc died," he said.

Might as well get this over with. "I became a librarian because I like learning. I can see or read something once and have it down cold. I've always been that way."

"A handy talent, especially when you're in school."

"Yes. It is. I attended boarding school in the first grade. Well, not exactly. I went to first grade for about two weeks, which was just enough time for the school to give the students IQ tests and get the results back. I tested very well and because of my test scores, I was offered several scholarships. My parents selected the scholarship offered by Brendan Academy. I started the fifth grade a few weeks later."

"Your parents didn't have a problem sending their six-year-old away to school?"

"My parents chose to send me to one of the best schools in the country for gifted students." That was the standard answer she'd learned to give while growing up. It hadn't helped when she first arrived. She'd cried herself to sleep at night, wondering what she'd done to make her parents send her away.

"If it were your child, would you make the same choice?" he asked.

"No. I got a great education but I missed out on a lot of other things." Like birthday parties with kids her own age and going out on dates. Maybe if she'd dated more, she would have realized Marc wasn't right for her before she married him.

"Marc thought my parents made the right decision. If we had children, he wanted them to go there. Start a new tradition. But I told him the only way my children would attend is if we'd moved close to the school so our child could come home every day."

"That sounds reasonable." It's what her parents should have done for her.

"Thanks. Truthfully I don't think we would have had children, even if he hadn't had a vasectomy. Marc was rarely home and when he was, he was usually working."

"Did he have friends at work?"

"He never mentioned anyone in particular other than his assistant, Bill Reynolds. They were in constant contact."

"Reynolds," he said, then turned in his chair and began typing on his laptop. "Marc wrote several checks to Bill Reynolds."

"He did?" She walked to his desk and looked over his shoulder at his computer screen. Marc had written fifteen checks to Reynolds in a period of three months. She sucked in her breath. "That's seven thousand six hundred and fifty-eight dollars and ninety-eight cents. What was Marc paying him to do?"

Chris thought that was a good question. He also wondered how she'd added up the sums of those checks so quickly in her head. He'd come back to that later. "We need to talk to Mr. Reynolds."

"Marc gave me his telephone number. I'll get it." She marched to her computer.

"It would be better to talk to him in person. Can you take off from work this week?"

"That's not a problem. My next contract with the library doesn't start until next month."

"Have you collected Marc's personal items from his office?"

"No. Mr. Reynolds said I could get them anytime."

"Perfect. Make an appointment to pick them up, but let him think you're coming alone. If Marc was paying him that much money, he knows something. I plan to find out what it is."

Chapter 8

Renee had no trouble making an appointment to meet with Bill Reynolds the following morning. They'd paid through the nose for round-trip tickets from Birmingham to Los Angeles, scheduled to depart the following morning. From the scant information he'd been able to find, Reynolds seemed to be your typical, middle-class employee. He had one speeding ticket last year and no criminal record.

Without Reynolds's bank records, Chris had no way of knowing what he did with the money. If this were a case, he would have gotten that information.

The amount of information Renee had gathered had him shaking his head in wonder. Most of the information was a matter of public record, but the average person wouldn't know where to find it.

"How did you learn to do all this?" he asked when the information just kept coming.

"I worked as an intern for an information brokerage firm. The company did everything from running background checks on potential employees to competitive analysis. My mentor was one of the best in the company. I almost accepted a position there when I finished library school, but I decided to get my Ph.D. instead."

"So, *that's* how you found all the information on Marc." He smiled. If she were with the bureau, she'd be hell on wheels and he'd probably have to fight off agents left and right to get to her. She fascinated him.

She gave him a puzzled look. "I told you that yesterday." At that moment her computer beeped. "Alex sent me an e-mail," she said, then gasped in disbelief.

"What?"

"Look at this." She turned the laptop around. "She used a purple font and it's from her work e-mail account," she said, stunned.

Chris didn't know what amused him more: the girly-girl purple font Alex used in her e-mail or Renee's shocked reaction. "Her family does own the company," he offered.

She looked at him as if he'd lost his mind. "A family-owned business is still a business. Who's going to take her seriously if she sends e-mails that look like this?"

"Maybe she doesn't want to be taken seriously." Alex had been called the black Paris Hilton for her party-girl lifestyle.

"Oh, trust me. She wants to be taken seriously." Renee picked up her cell phone and seconds later had Alex on the line.

While Renee talked to Alex about correct business correspondence, he read the e-mail message. Alex knew nothing about the necklace, but would ask a friend of a friend who was really into estate jewelry if she'd seen a necklace like that lately.

He doubted her friend of a friend would have seen the necklace. Most of Alex's crowd was constantly in celebrity magazines. It would not be good for them to be photographed wearing stolen jewelry. For the past year, Alex had kept a low profile, no doubt due to Marc's influence. He'd learned how to dodge the press from Danielle.

He watched her pace from one end of the office to the next. She seemed to know a lot about Alex's company. "Alex, stop second-guessing yourself." Renee put her hand on her hip. "Your business plans are fine. Wait, someone's on the other line. Hang on a second." She looked at the phone. "It's Danielle. I'm going to put us on three-way."

A few minutes later, Renee closed the phone. "Marc didn't give the necklace to either of them," she said.

"It was a long shot, but at least we know they don't have it.

"Yeah. I would have been really ticked off if Marc had given it to either of them. I still don't understand why he took the necklace."

"Money."

"That's just it. He wouldn't accept the money Aunt Gert wanted to give us as a wedding present. He wouldn't even move into this house because he didn't want her to lose the income she got by renting it. It doesn't make sense."

"Things don't always make sense, especially when Marc is involved. He didn't have to steal, but he was really good at shoplifting when we were growing up."

"What? Are you serious?"

"Dead serious. I think the only reason he wasn't caught is that we moved all the time. If we lived someplace for more than a year, store security would follow us around. They knew one of us was stealing, but they never caught him."

"Did they catch you?" she asked softly.

"I never stole anything. I got caught trying to return a watch Marc had stolen." Even now his stomach burned with anger and frustration. "He'd stolen a Rolex to give to Mom for her birthday. I told him to take it back because she'd get in trouble. She worked as a maid in a hotel and she'd cleaned a few houses for extra money. If she'd shown up at work wearing that watch, they would have accused her of stealing it. He wouldn't take it back. He said it was time Mom had something nice. I took the watch back to the store but I got caught with it in my pocket."

"How old were you?"

"Ten. They didn't press charges against me because I didn't have a record and when they reviewed the security video, they saw that I didn't go in the area where the watches were sold. We ended up leaving because she couldn't get extra work. Nobody wanted to hire a maid who was the mother of a thief."

"I'm sorry," she said softly.

"I don't need your sympathy. You need to understand that Marc was more than capable of stealing."

It was darn hard trying to sneak glances at Chris while driving on I-459 to have dinner with Aunt Gert. Renee had driven to the bank where Aunt Gert's safe-deposit box was located. Chris copied the dates from the log of the box.

He hadn't said much since he told her about Marc stealing a Rolex. Her heart ached for the ten-year-old boy who'd tried to do the right thing and had it blow up in his face.

He was a walking anomaly. He could have easily become a thief like his brother, but there was a core of honor and justice that prevailed inside of him. She realized now that if she'd come to him when she'd learned the necklace was gone, he would have helped her. Because helping her was the right thing to do.

She'd done all she could to block him when he was trying be fair to the wives, and she'd used Marc's actions as an excuse to treat him with distrust. No, she couldn't put all the blame on Marc for the way she treated him. Chris was handsome, sexy and powerful. The attraction she felt for him shook her so she had acted like a jerk. He didn't deserve it.

As she drove into the parking garage of the condominium complex, she considered apologizing to him, but didn't. If she apologized, then she'd have to explain why. There was no way she was telling him that she was attracted to him. No way.

She would just have to be nice to him and put a damper on her attraction. It shouldn't be hard. After all, he'd only be here for two weeks.

Chris scanned the lobby with its tan plastered walls and pristine-white columns as he rolled what Renee had called a scrapbook bag along the gleaming earth-tone terrazzo floor. The bag was shaped like a square, stumpy suitcase and weighed a ton. When they were leaving her house, they had a brief tug-of-war over the case. The war didn't last long. He'd simply picked up the case and walked out the door. She'd had no choice but to follow.

Classical music played softly in the background. The building had elegance and money written all over it. A number of large, plush sofas and chairs where scattered around the area separated by large green plants. On one of the sofas, three older men looked up from behind newspapers. One man smiled when he saw Renee and all three gave him a hard, assessing look.

Renee shifted one of the two plastic grocery bags in one hand and waved to the group. The three men nodded hello, but didn't make any attempt to start reading their papers again. Chris positioned himself so he had a clear view of them. Something in the way they looked at him made him suspicious.

Renee walked to a large desk. Standing behind it was an older white man with thinning gray hair, wearing a black three-piece suit and a condescending look, and a young Hispanic uniformed security guard.

"Good evening, Mrs. Foster. What do you have in the bags?" The man's pompous tone grated on his nerves.

"Groceries," she replied. "I still haven't received a copy of the amended homeowners' agreement, Mr. Hall."

The smile the man gave her was smug. "I'm sure the home office has mailed it. You should have it soon. May I?" He held out his hand.

Renee placed the bags on the counter. The man looked inside then turned to Chris. "Please sign the visitors' sign-in sheet."

Chris signed his name on the paper and followed Renee to the elevator and maneuvered the bag inside when the doors opened.

"What was that all about?"

She frowned. "About a month ago, Aunt Gert received a memo stating a change had been made to the homeowners' agreement. Now, residents and visitors are allowed to bring two bottles of alcohol on the premises per day. Aunt Gert never received a copy of the new agreement. I asked Mr. Hall about it and he said contact the home office."

"Is he the manager?"

"Yes."

"Seems like an arrogant son of..."

"Shush." She held her finger to her lips.

"Gun," he added drily. "I do try to watch my language around you."

"Thanks."

"You don't swear at all?" He had never met anyone outside of preachers who didn't curse.

"No...well, okay. I did say two bad words when I went to the safe-deposit box and discovered Aunt Gert's necklace missing." Her face was red and she looked down at her feet.

Chris grinned. "Did anybody hear you?"

"No. I was alone." Her face grew redder.

He waited until she looked at him. "What did you say?"

Her mouth dropped for a few seconds. "I'm not...I'm not..." she sputtered, pursed her lips, then straightened her shoulders. "No."

"How about if I guess?"

The elevator doors opened and she walked down the hall without answering him. He knew what he would have said if he'd been in her situation, and he wouldn't have stopped at two words, but now he burned with curiosity to know what she'd said.

She stopped in front of a brown door. To the right was a speaker panel with the number 323, and a glowing doorbell. She pressed the button.

Gertrude Alma Lee Mitchell wore her silver-gray hair in short curls that framed her dark brown skin. Her dark brown eyes were filled with curiosity and intelligence. She looked sixty but his file listed her age as eighty-eight.

"Come on in." Her voice was strong and she spoke with a slow, melodious rhythm.

"Aunt Gert," Renee said, "this is Christopher Foster, Marc's younger brother. Chris, this is my great-aunt, Ms. Gertrude Mitchell."

Chris let go of the handle and shook the older woman's hand. "Nice to meet you, Ms. Mitchell." She wore a plain blue dress with pearl earrings and a watch with a thin black band, its geometric face set in diamonds.

"Nice to meet you, as well, and please, call me Miss Gert. Renee, put those bags in the kitchen. Mr. Foster, you can leave that—" she pointed to the rolling bag "—over in the corner."

"Chris, please," he said.

Renee gave the bag a furtive glance and walked to the other side of the room to the kitchen area. A half wall screened the kitchen from view. He looked down at the bag. *What's in the bag?*

"Please, have a seat." Ms. Mitchell touched his arm and motioned toward the seating area.

The place reminded him of an old black and white Hollywood movie with its sophisticated art deco style. Gertrude Mitchell was a wealthy woman and it showed in her jewelry and furniture. He sat down in a curved leather armchair.

"Dinner will be ready in a few minutes." She sat on the sofa in front of him. "Have you been to Birmingham before, Chris?"

"Only once," he replied.

"Aunt Gert, I'm going to put your mouthwash in the hall pantry." Renee held one of the bags in her hand and grabbed the handle of the rolling bag. "I'll take this to the extra bedroom." She raced out of the room. What the hell was going on with the bag? He remembered the man searching her bag but he never looked in the rolling bag and then it came to him. Chris grinned. She was smuggling in alcohol in a scrapbook case.

"So you're Marc's brother," Miss Gert said.

"I am," he said as Renee joined her great-aunt on the sofa, looking a little anxious.

"Well," Miss Gert said. "He didn't mention a word about you. Why is that?"

Chris studied the woman in front of him. She had a mildly curious look on her face, but the look in her eyes had him thinking that he wasn't getting out of here without answering her question.

"Marc and I haven't been close for many years. Did you get a chance to know him?"

"Somewhat. He traveled a lot, but he did make time to see me when he was home. If you weren't close, why did he make you executor? It seems to me that he would have made Renee the executor?"

"Aunt Gert, really," Renee said with some distress.

"No. She's got a point," he said. "I think he made me the executor because he knew I would make sure that everything was done right."

She raised her brows. "Oh, are you a lawyer?"

"No. I'm with law enforcement."

"Which branch?"

"Aunt Gert," Renee gasped. "Did you invite us to dinner so you could pump him for information?" Renee looked aghast.

"Of course."

He laughed. He had to admire a woman who wasn't shy about getting what she wanted. "It's all right, Renee. I'm with the FBI, Miss Gert."

"Oh. Well, I must confess. I was concerned when Renee told me about you. Marc never mentioned you and suddenly there you are. But you're with the FBI so he must have reason to trust you."

"So it would seem," he replied. "The last time I saw Marc, I realized that I really didn't know him. I've talked to Renee about him but I'd like to hear what you thought of Marc."

"Marc was such a charming man. He didn't say much about his people, though." She looked at him.

"Who are your people? Are they all from California?"

"I really don't know much about my family. My father didn't have family and my mother's family died before I was born. That's probably why Marc didn't talk about them," he said. He believed the real reason Marc didn't talk about his family was that he didn't want people to know too much about him. If they knew too much then he could be caught in his lies.

"So California is your home," Miss Gert said.

"No, California is where I was born. I live in Atlanta for now."

"For now," Renee said. "Are you moving?"

"Yes. Probably to Washington, D.C."

"You don't like Atlanta?" Miss Gert asked.

"It's fine. I move about every two years for my job. Which is one of the reasons why Marc and I didn't keep in touch."

"The two of you have that in common. Marc traveled for his job a lot. He could talk to anyone. I guess you'd need that talent to be a good salesman. And he was always willing to help. He would run little errands for me. I keep a running list of things I need to do. I don't remember things like I used to."

"That's not true," Renee said with a laugh. "You remember everything."

"No. I write things down and keep good records. It surprises people when I repeat what they told me months ago. It keeps them on their toes and honest.

Marc told me he was going to follow my example and write everything down."

"Did he?" Chris prompted. He hoped Marc had written down where he'd taken the necklace.

"I'm sure he did. He always had file folders in his briefcase. He even showed me the folder he had on me."

"He had a folder on you?" Renee asked in surprise.

"Yes, and he probably had one on you, too," she said and patted Renee's hand. "He gave me a copy of my file. He wanted to make sure he hadn't forgotten anything."

"Forgotten what?"

"All kinds of things." She stopped at the sound of a timer and stood. "We can talk about this over dinner."

"I'll get it." Renee jumped out of her seat before either of them could, and went to the kitchen.

"Do you want help with that?" he offered.

"Save your breath, young man," Miss Gert told him. "Renee's not letting either of us in there."

"That's right," Renee said, bringing out a large covered dish. "I can handle this." She walked back to the kitchen.

"Renee won't let me lift a finger to do anything if she's here. It's sweet." She smiled then whispered, "I sneak and do stuff anyway."

He chuckled at the mischievous expression on her face. "I won't tell her," he said softly.

Renee set another dish on the table. "Dinner's ready."

Dinner consisted of smothered pork chops, real homemade mashed potatoes, fat string beans that Miss Gert called pole beans, fried corn, homemade dinner rolls and a drink called Arnold Palmer, which was half sweet tea and half lemonade. The small dinette table barely had enough room for all the food, which was excellent.

"Renee was right," he said after the first bite of his pork chop. "You are a great cook."

"Why, thank you. Save room for dessert. It's Renee's favorite—peach cobbler."

"I will." He took a few more bites of his meal and turned the conversation back to Marc. "So did Marc have in his file that you were a good cook?"

She smiled. "No, nothing like that. It had my birthday, my favorite perfume, my favorite wine. You know, little things about me."

"That must have been a very small file," he said.

"Yes, it was. The biggest thing was the list of errands he'd done for me."

"I would have run your errands for you," Renee said.

Although she tried to disguise it, he recognized the underlying hurt in her tone. He wasn't the only one who heard it.

"I know, sugar, but I think this was his way of getting to know you better."

Renee frowned. "What do mean?"

"He used the errands as an excuse to talk to me about you. You don't talk about your childhood. That part of your life you keep to yourself. We'd look at the pictures I had of you growing up and I'd tell him about you."

Chris nodded. It was also a good way to get her to trust him. Marc wasn't dumb. Anyone who'd been around the two women could see that they loved each other. Gertrude Mitchell may be Renee's great-aunt, but she treated Renee like a treasured granddaughter.

"Do you have a lot of pictures of Renee?" he asked.

She smiled. "Of course, would you like to see them?"

"Oh, but…" Renee protested.

"I'd love to," he said over her objections.

"But what about dessert?" Renee said.

"Dessert will still be here when we finish looking at the pictures," her great-aunt said, getting to her feet. "I'll get the file, too."

They went back to the living room. He sat on the sofa next to the older woman. She'd retrieved three large photo albums from a small cabinet. She opened the first album. "This one is my favorite."

Renee, sporting pigtails and bangs, sat next to Gertrude on a sofa. Renee's lips turned up slightly at the corners and Gertrude had her arm around her small shoulders. In the background was a large Christmas tree decorated with glass ornaments and

white lights, but it was the diamond necklace
around Renee's neck that caught his attention.
"That's quite a necklace," he said.

"It's very special to me. Renee's the only person
who I will allow to wear it. This was our first Christmas together. We were having our own private
party. A girl can't go to a party without her fine
jewelry," she said then smiled gently. "Now, we
have a party every Christmas for just the two of us."

He studied the photo closely. Gertrude's smile
was wide and bright. She wore the matching earrings and a diamond and pearl necklace. But it was
Renee's smile that drew his attention. There was an
underlying sadness in her shy smile, and he wondered what had put it there.

"How old was she here?"

"Six, and just as cute as a button and as curious
as three kittens."

The age she'd started boarding school. *Where the
hell were her parents?* He looked across the room
at Renee who looked uncomfortable with the discussion. "Curious about what?" he asked.

"That year, she wanted to know all about mining
for diamonds. She wanted to go to Africa so she
could find diamonds for her own necklace, until she
learned all the mines were privately owned. Then
she started looking at designers. We must have
checked out all the books in the library on jewels."

"Has the necklace been in your family long?" he
asked.

"No. It was a gift from the man I loved. He'd gone to New York and came back with the necklace and earrings. He said it was a bribe to get me to marry him."

"You didn't want to marry him?" Chris asked intrigued.

"Oh, I wanted to marry him, but things were complicated with him. I didn't like complications. He did know how to impress a woman and he'd had it designed just for me."

"I didn't know that," Renee said. "I always thought it was a Cartier."

"No. Paul Laveau created my necklace. He was Creole and tried to make it as a designer in New York in the 1930s. For a time, he was the premiere designer for wealthy African-Americans. He moved to France after a few years. I wanted to have another piece of jewelry designed by him, but no one knew where to find him."

"I could try to find information for you," Renee offered.

She looked at Renee with surprise. "Well, I thought you had. Marc said the Laveau family is still making jewelry in France. He said you found the information for him."

Chris felt his gut clench. This didn't sound good.

"I don't remember," Renee said.

"Well, don't worry about it. He said the jewelry they produce now looks nothing like my necklace. He went to their store in Paris early this year and showed them a picture of the necklace and earrings, but they told him they'd moved away from that type of design." She sighed. "What a shame."

"Aunt Gert, you let Marc take one of your pictures?"

"No, I had him get the negatives from the safe-deposit box. Oh, and I need you to get the necklace for me. I plan to wear it to the dance next week."

Chapter 9

How in the world were they going to find the necklace in a week? Renee was startled when Chris answered. She hadn't realized she'd spoken aloud.

"We can start by finding out why Marc was so interested in Laveau," he said.

"I've been trying to remember if he asked me to research the name. It does sound familiar," she said.

"He didn't put that information in the folder he gave Miss Gert."

She'd been surprised by the number of errands Marc had run for Aunt Gert. It was one more thing she hadn't known about him. There was no reference to the necklace in the folder.

When they were back at her house, it didn't take Renee long to find the jewelry store owned by the Laveau family.

"La Belle Fleur. I vaguely remember doing a search for jewelry stores in Paris, but Marc said it was for business. His company had developed some sort of plastic they were going to sell to jewelry makers for molds." She sent the information to the printer, which immediately began spitting out pages. She watched Chris go to the printer and lift the pages as they rolled out.

It was hard to keep her mind on the task when she'd been distracted by the sight of his very fine behind. She couldn't help it. He really turned her on with his sexy body and sharp mind. She'd been around more than her fair share of brilliant men, but Chris had something more. He had a casual assurance that made you believe he could do anything he put his mind to, and do it well. She wished he was as attracted to her as she was to him. He wasn't and there was no use thinking about it. Think about the necklace.

Watching him with Aunt Gert had been an education. She knew he was fishing for information, but he'd done it with a light touch. He'd made it seem like he was just having conversation and she doubted if Aunt Gert noticed. He'd also kept his word and not told her the necklace was gone. She was grateful for that.

"Marc went to Paris three months before he took

the necklace." Chris collected the pages and brought the printout to her, then sat on the edge of the desk. "He didn't go back to France before he died. I don't see a strong enough connection between his trip to France and the designer."

She kept her gaze on his face, trying to think of him as a coworker. It didn't really work. "He went to a lot of trouble for nothing," she said in frustration. They were no closer to finding the necklace now than before they spoke with Aunt Gert.

"It wasn't a lot of trouble. Marc was looking for something. I don't think he found it in Paris." He looked at the large whiteboard where they'd added Marc's trip to Paris to the list of places Marc had been within the last six months.

"Why not?"

"Miss Gert knew he was looking for information on Laveau. He was too cunning not to have covered his tracks."

Renee remembered how well Marc had covered his tracks with three wives. Yeah, he was cunning all right. "So, we've got nothing."

He looked at her. "No. When we talk to Bill Reynolds tomorrow, we'll see what he knows about Laveau and the necklace. We know Marc was looking for something or else he would have taken the necklace sooner. Find out what he was looking for and find the necklace." He looked so calm, so confident and so unbelievably sexy.

She looked at her laptop. *Focus, Renee, focus.*

"You're right. I just wish…" She shrugged her shoulders. "It doesn't matter."

"What is it that you wish?" His voice was smooth, rich like her favorite blend of coffee.

There were so many things she wished. She wished the necklace was in the safe-deposit box where it belonged. She wished she was the kind of woman he wanted. She wished she could change whatever it was about her that made her unlovable. Renee rubbed her eyes. Wishing didn't change anything. She'd have to stop wishing for the impossible and concentrate on what she could do something about. "I wish Marc had taken something of mine instead of Aunt Gert's."

"I know. She really loves that necklace." He leaned forward, bringing his face closer to hers.

She felt her pulse jump, then race. He was so close that all she had to do was lean forward to kiss his lips. She was not going to kiss him and she wasn't going to blush. She wasn't. She leaned back in her chair and…dang it, started blushing.

"I think you should tell her," he said.

It took a few seconds for her to register what he'd said. She shook her head. "No. I'm…"

"Hear me out before you say no." He interrupted. "Miss Gert is a strong woman and she loves you very much. I think she'll be angry and hurt, but she'll put the blame where it needs to be, which is on Marc."

There was such certainty in his expression, but this was too important. "I can't tell her."

"At least tell her about the robbery before she finds out some other way," he said.

She stared at him in horror. "Ohmygod! I forgot to tell her." She grabbed the phone and quickly dialed Aunt Gert's number. When the answering machine kicked on, she hung up and called the cell phone. She breathed a sigh of relief when she heard Aunt Gert's voice.

Ten minutes later, Renee felt drained. She'd talked Aunt Gert out of driving over to see her. She'd danced around the truth several times during their conversation and she'd flat-out lied about the reason they were in the store. She hated to lie. It made her stomach hurt.

"You should have let me talk to her," Chris said. He'd listened to the entire conversation.

"Why?" She wondered why he was looking at her with a grin on his face.

"You should have told her you were in the jewelry store and you left out the reason why," he said. "You're a rotten liar."

She frowned at him. "I don't think that's a bad thing. Lies can hurt people."

"Some lies hurt. Sometimes the truth hurts," he said calmly. "You're letting Marc's lies control you. Miss Gert loves you. Tell her the truth. You've got nothing to lose."

She stood and the level of her frustration rose with her. *She didn't have anything to lose?* "I know she loves me. You want to know why? I do everything in my power to make her happy. If she wants beets for lunch then guess what? Beets for lunch it is. I hate beets but I'd eat a refrigerator full of them for her."

He came to his feet and said softly, "She knows you'd do anything for her and that's all the more reason to tell her. She gave Marc access to her safe deposit."

"You don't get it." She shook her head. How could he understand? With his looks and personality, he never had to worry about being alone. He never had to wonder what he'd done to make his parents not love him like she had. "She made me responsible for her necklace, not my parents, not her lawyer, but me. She has certain expectations of me and I'm not going to disappoint her. Ever."

"Are you saying that you can't make a mistake? That's crazy. You're not perfect. Nobody's perfect."

"I don't want to be perfect, just the woman she expects me to be."

"So you put on a performance for her and never let her see the real you? Isn't that the same thing Marc did to you?"

His words were like hard, stinging blows. "No! I don't steal. I don't cheat."

"Yes, you do. You're cheating yourself and Miss Gert out of the real Renee Foster. Why are you so afraid to be yourself?"

"I'm being myself." But even as she spoke, she began to doubt her own words.

"Where are your diplomas?"

"My diplomas? What do they have to do with anything?"

"Tell me where they are."

She shook her head in confusion. "They're in a box in the hall closet."

"So you're hiding them, too?"

"I'm not hiding anything. Where do you come off telling me this? You don't know me at all."

His smile was slow, dark and sexy. "Oh, I know you," he said, then walked toward her. "I know you're stubborn. You're smart…"

She took a step back. Her stomach felt fluttery like she'd crested the highest hill of a roller coaster and was about to take a plunge. He looked at her as if he could see something within her that no one else had. Her pulse began to race as he continued to speak, drawing closer and closer until he was standing in front of her.

"…you're loyal and you're sexy as hell." His tone was deep and seductive.

His subtle, masculine scent filled her senses and she found it hard to breathe. "You're lying."

Slowly he lowered his head until his lips were but a whisper away from her own. "Renee," he whispered. "I never lie about sexy." He turned his head and kissed her cheek.

Her eyes widened in surprise as he left a trail of warm, lingering kisses down her cheek to the edge of her mouth. His lips lingered on her skin in a slow, seductive dance. With his tongue, he touched the edge of her mouth and she felt her nipples harden and contract as if he'd caressed them. Her breath quickened and she parted her lips and ached with anticipation.

His body was close, so close, and yet he used only his lips to touch, taste and caress her. Desire flowed through her, making her vividly aware of the heat radiating from his body. She shivered with longing as he rubbed his cheek against hers, loving the hard, rough feel of his jaw against her skin. He made her feel special, wanted and desired.

He pulled back and studied her. His gaze went to her mouth and the hunger in his eyes was hot, raw and intense. She felt her knees shake. She wanted to feel his lips on hers, feel his hard body next to hers. She wanted.

They stood almost touching for a few long seconds then Renee met his hot, patient gaze. In an instant, she understood what he wanted.

She closed the tiny distance that separated them. Wrapping her arms around his waist, pressing her body against his, she felt the hard length of him. Then, as if he'd been waiting for her touch, he pressed his lips to hers. She parted her lips and welcomed his tongue. She tasted a hint of peach cobbler on his lips. The combination of Chris and peach cobbler went to her head like a shot of finely aged rum. Her heart raced as her tongue mated with his. She groaned in protest when he ended the kiss.

"Renee." His voice was deep and husky.

Slowly she opened her eyes and met his heated gaze.

"I want you," he said. His words made her tremble with desire. "I want the real Renee Mitchell Foster." He stepped back and out of their embrace. "When you're ready to let her out, let me know. She's the woman I want." He took another step back, turned and walked out of the room.

Renee stood in shocked silence, watching him leave. He was just going to leave? He got her all worked up and he was leaving?

A few seconds later, anger and hurt replaced the shock and she began pacing. Who did he think he was? She knew exactly who she was. She was Renee Mitchell Foster. She lived in *this* house because she wanted to live here permanently. She'd decorated it the way she'd wanted. So what if her diplomas were packed in a box—they were hers and she could do anything she wanted with them. She stopped. Couldn't she? Dread settled in the pit of her stomach. Her diplomas had been hanging on the wall in her den and for the first time, she'd had them all displayed until her parents had come through town.

"Why do you have them all here? One or two are fine but this—" Her mother motioned to the wall. "This won't do. Aunt Gert's home was always polished. What's she going to think when she sees this?"

She'd taken them down that day. Renee walked

to her chair and sat down. She'd worked darn hard to earn each and every one of her diplomas, but she'd packed them in a box and put them in the closet because she was afraid her mother was right.

Okay, she was definitely hiding things from Aunt Gert concerning Marc and the necklace. She had a valid reason for it, but her diplomas? She realized she didn't really have a reason to keep them in the closet. It didn't mean she was hiding who she was or that she didn't know who she was. It meant... She slumped in the chair. It meant that Chris had a point. She'd copped out and done something to please her mother, not what she really wanted. Wasn't it time to do exactly what she wanted for a change?

"Yes," she said. "Yes, it is." She walked out of her office and down the hall to the closet. It didn't take her long to drag the box out of the closet and into the den. She peeled back the packing tape and opened the box. Carefully, she removed each of the framed diplomas and leaned them against the wall. She wouldn't hang them up tonight, but she would hang them.

How had he known? No one other than her mother had mentioned her diplomas, yet Chris had not only noticed but understood what their lack of appearance meant. She'd moved here because this was where she wanted to be. Turning it into her home had been her mission when she'd learned of Marc's deception. For the most part she'd done it.

Everything was as she wanted it to be except for this one wall. What else had she copped out on?

She turned and screamed. Chris stood in the hall watching her as silent and still as a panther stalking its prey.

"Where did you come from?" she asked, pressing a hand to her chest, feeling the rapid pounding of her heart. It wasn't fear alone that made her heart race.

"Upstairs," he replied as he walked into the den. "I didn't mean to scare you."

How had he gone up the stairs and come down them without her hearing him? She lowered her hand. "Well, you did."

"I apologize." He went to the wall where she'd placed her diplomas. "Do you need help with these?"

She started to say no, but then shrugged her shoulders. She'd planned on hanging them anyway. "Sure. Why not?" She went into the kitchen pantry where she kept a toolbox.

With Chris's help, they had the diplomas on the wall in no time. She took a step back and looked at the wall. "I like them better hanging than in the closet."

"They look good," he said.

She kept her gaze on the wall. If she didn't look at him then maybe she could say what needed to be said. "I'm the odd duck in the family, at school, even at work. I'm not like everyone else so I have to work really hard to even come close to fitting in. I'm never going to fit in but it's easier for everyone if I let people see who they want to see."

Out the corner of her eye, she saw him turn to face her. She couldn't look at him. Not yet.

"But that's not the real you," he said.

"A lot of times it is, but sometimes it's not. No one has ever wanted to see the real me."

"I do," he said softly.

She closed her eyes. His words warmed a part of her heart that she'd closed off years ago. She turned to him and saw honesty shining in his pale brown eyes and realized she wanted to be totally honest with him. "Okay. I'll be honest with you but you've got to be honest with me, too."

"I'll be as honest as I can. There are some things that I can't or won't tell you, but I won't lie to you."

"That's fair." She grasped her hands suddenly, not sure what to do with herself. "So how does this work? Do we ask questions of each other? Tell each other stories about our past? What?"

He smiled. "It doesn't matter to me. Why don't you decide how you want it to work."

It was hard to think when he smiled at her like that. He personified everything masculine and strong. From his broad shoulders to his long, muscular thighs, he was her greatest temptation. "We'll ask questions. I guess." For the life of her she couldn't think of a single question that didn't involve sex in some way. Her very analytical mind was more accustomed to remembering mathematical theorems, and yet she remembered in vivid detail the feel of his lips on hers. "I don't know the right thing to ask you," she said, then remembered. "Oh, wait. I've got a book."

He raised a brow. "A book."

"Yes. Hold on. I'll get it." She hurried down the hall to the library. The book would make it easier for her to ask questions and hopefully keep her occupied enough to control the powerful attraction she felt for him. She found the book and returned to stand in front of him. "Here it is," she said, holding up the book so he could see the title.

"Ten Thousand Great Questions," he said, meeting her gaze. "Are you serious?"

"We don't have to ask them all."

Deadpan, he said, "Thank God."

"Here." She opened the book and flipped a few pages. "I'll start with an easy one. What's your favorite color?"

"Blue," he said with no hesitation.

"Mine is emerald-green."

"I've never seen you wear that color. Everything I've seen you wear has been black or white."

"Most of my clothes are black, white or a combination of the two. It's easier for me." She held out the book. "Your turn."

He shook his head and said coolly, calmly, "Thanks, but I don't need the book to ask my question."

She frowned. "You don't?" Then she remembered where he worked. "FBI. Right, I forgot." She walked to the sofa and sat down. Her stomach felt jumpy. She was almost as nervous now as she'd been in Terrell's office.

"Do you want me?"

Her eyes widened with surprise. Why couldn't he have started with an easier question? The nervousness she'd felt moments before was nothing compared to what she felt now. Memories of past rejections and old fears had her mouth going suddenly dry. She turned her head and stared into the empty fireplace.

Do you want me? It was such a simple question. Her answer would change everything between them. This she knew for certain. She folded her hands together and resisted the urge to run rather than expose the truth. She had to tell him the truth. He deserved the truth. She took a deep breath to steady her nerves and gather her courage. She turned to meet his waiting gaze and said, "Yes. I do."

He stared at her with heat and longing in his gaze. "Good, because I very much want you." He lowered his gaze to her mouth and her lips began to tingle in response. "Your turn," he said.

She watched his lips move. The husky bass of his voice sent warm, lingering heat through her body. It took her a few seconds to register what he'd said. "My...my turn?"

His gazed moved from her lips, down her throat to her breasts before slowly making the return up past her lips and into her eyes. "Your turn to ask a question," he said.

Question. Huh? She struggled to bring her scrambled senses in order. "I...um...I need to tell you something first."

"All right," he said and put his hands in his pockets.

Her gaze instantly went below his waist where his erection tented the front of his pants. Embarrassed, she quickly looked up at his face. His half smile and knowing look sent heat rushing to her face. Determined to have her say, she kept her eyes on his face. "If you...we—" She stopped and collected herself. "If we are going to sleep together, then you should know that I'm not really good at sex. I like the kissing." She hurried on, trying to say it all before she chickened out. "And the touching, but the act itself just doesn't do it for me. But I'd like to have sex with you, if you want to."

Chapter 10

Chris had a curious look on his face. Not quite frowning and not quite smiling…somewhere in the middle. Renee didn't know what to make of it. At least he hadn't laughed at her, or worse, looked disgusted by her admission.

"The act doesn't do it for you." He said it as though he was talking to himself.

She swallowed. She wasn't sure if she should respond to him because he hadn't asked her a question, so she didn't. He watched her with that puzzled expression on his face for a few seconds. Waiting made her want to squirm. *Why didn't he answer her question? Had he changed his mind?*

Then he nodded. "I definitely want to sleep with you, and just so you know, you're safe with me. I always use protection."

She let out the breath she didn't know she'd been holding. Relieved that he hadn't changed his mind. "I'm on the pill and I got a full physical when I came back from the funeral, so I'm healthy." She felt a little awkward talking to him about protection, but at the same time she felt reassured by his consideration. She felt confident he would be just as considerate in her bed and she looked forward to kissing him again, feeling his hands on her body.

He walked to the sofa. Looking at her with such heated focus that made her even more aroused. "I want to sleep with you now. If that's okay with you."

She couldn't control the shiver of desire that ran through her at his words. "It's okay with me."

He held out his hand, she accepted it and stood. He brought her palm to his lips and kissed it. Fiery sensation traveled up her arm, down her chest and between her legs. He threaded his fingers through hers. "Let's go upstairs."

All she could do was nod; he'd taken her breath away. They climbed the stairs and when they'd reached the top, he motioned for her to lead the way. Her knees felt shaky as she held his hand and walked down the short hallway to her bedroom. She'd never led a man to her bedroom and she found the experience exciting. When they reached her bedroom door, he stopped her.

"Wait here. I'll be right back," he said, letting go of her hand and walking down the hall to the extra bedroom.

She watched in confusion as he left, but did what he asked, and then she understood. A few seconds later, he returned empty-handed. He saw the look on her face.

"Condoms," he said.

"Where?" she asked, looking at his empty hands.

He smiled and lifted her into his arms. "Pants pockets." He kissed her softly. "Shirt pocket." He carried her inside her bedroom.

She wrapped an arm around his shoulder and put her other hand on his chest, moving her hand slowly across the cotton dress shirt until she found the pocket. She reached inside and pulled out four sealed packets. "Are we going to need four?"

"No. I'll go easy on you this time." He set her on her feet beside her bed. The lamp on her night-stand cast a warm glow in the room.

She tilted her head. "What do you mean?"

"Why don't I show you." He unfastened the clip holding her ponytail and tossed it on her night-stand. "You have pretty hair, Renee." He threaded his fingers through her locks, spreading it on her shoulders, and gently massaging her scalp. "I've wanted to do this for a long time."

His hands felt wonderful, but she wanted something more. "Can I do something?"

He ran his hands over her hair then cupped her

face. "You can do whatever you'd like, wherever you'd like."

She stepped aside and put the condoms beside her lamp. "I want to take off your shirt," she said in a voice she barely recognized, and took his wrist and unbuttoned one sleeve, then the other.

He stood there watching as she hurriedly unfastened the buttons on the front of his shirt then pushed it off his shoulders, down his arms, and let it drop to the floor. He dressed like a high-level executive. Looking at his chest made her mouth water. He had the look of a man who had gotten his muscles by doing long, hard, physical labor. His arms and shoulders were lean and tight. There was a light dusting of hair, but it was the dark line of hair that bisected his carved abs that made her want to follow its path down and below.

"I really like your chest," she said, enjoying the view.

"I am glad y—" He stopped and sucked in his breath when she lifted her shirt over her head. Without hesitating, she released the front clasp of her bra, wrapped her arms around his shoulders. The feel of his hard, warm skin against her breasts was better than any fantasy. She closed her eyes, lifted to her tiptoes, groaning as she rubbed her nipples against his chest, up and down, over and over.

He put his hands on her shoulders, pulled back. "My turn," he said. Bending down, he kissed her lips, her chin, her neck, her shoulder, then brushed his lips down the slope of her breast. He closed his lips over her hardened nipple and sucked, licked and teased. Turning his head, he gave her other nipple the same treatment—licking, kissing one then the other until her whole body felt as if it were on fire.

She held his head, loving what he was doing to her. Her heart jumped in her throat when he bent lower and kissed her stomach. With adept hands, he loosened the button to her pants and slid the zipper down.

"Wait." She put her hands on his shoulders for balance and slipped off her shoes.

His hands went to the waistband and he slid her trouseres and her white panties down her legs. She stepped out of her clothes.

The cool air flowed over her heated skin. The sight of Chris kneeling in front of her, looking at her as if she were the most beautiful woman he'd ever seen, made her feel bold and sexy. She cupped his face in her hands and kissed him, hard, long and deep.

He wrapped his hands around her wrists and gently pulled away. He rose to his feet then swept her in his arms and laid her on the bed. He looked down at her. "You're beautiful."

He made her feel beautiful. "You don't look so bad yourself, even if you do have on too many clothes."

"Then it's time for them to come off," he said, his voice raw with desire.

A part of her regretted what was to come. She wanted to kiss him and touch him more. Be kissed and touched more. Her limited experience had taught her that men didn't enjoy that part of making love as much she did. She turned on her side and watched him get rid of his clothing.

"Oh, wow," was all she could say. Then he was there in the bed beside her, kissing her. His tongue slid between her lips, urging her to share his need. He guided her onto her back and kissed her neck. "Do you like when I kiss you, Renee?"

"Lord, yes," she gasped as he spread kisses down her neck to her breasts, and arched her back and gripped his shoulders in delight when he gently pressed his teeth on her nipple.

He licked her nipple and slid his hand between her legs, sending sharp bursts of pleasure through-out her body. Her hands fell to the mattress when his thumb gently stroked her warm, wet core, tempting, urging her toward a sweet, tingling sen-sation. His hands moved faster, pushing her closer and closer to release so sweet. Her shoulders and back tightened as swirls of heat became tighter and tighter until all she could do was close her eyes and moan as he suckled and kissed her breasts. A blinding sensation broke over her; she groaned, arched her back and moved her hips with abandon.

Later, when her body began to grow lax and her climax began to fade, Renee opened her eyes and met Chris's hot, sensual gaze.

"If I don't get inside you, I'll explode." He turned and grabbed a condom from the nightstand.

"I'm beat," she said, using all the energy she had to say the words.

"Don't worry. I've got something that will perk you up." He donned the condom and turned to her.

"I don't know," she said, feeling loose and boneless as he ran his fingers through her hair.

"I do. I'm going to touch and kiss every inch of your body," he said and kissed her brow. "Then I'm going watch as your eyes glaze with pleasure." He bit her earlobe.

She felt her body beginning to stir. "When do I get to kiss you all over?" She felt his erection flex against her hip and smiled.

He took her hand and placed it on his chest; his heart was pounding against her palm. "You can start here," he said, and groaned when she moved her thumb across his nipple.

She watched as his jaw tightened as she stroked and caressed him. Renewed energy flowed through her as she watched him. She kissed his neck; his groan sent pleasure down her spine. She wanted him. She longed to feel him between her legs, inside her.

He took her hand and placed it on his shoulder then ran the back of his hand down her chest, over her stomach and circling her navel.

"Chris." Her voice strained with pleasure as he sat up and moved his palm down the side of her hip and over her thigh to her knee. She tensed with anticipation when he turned his palm over the knee and began moving up the inside of her thigh. She opened her legs farther. He touched her, circling, pleasing.

"You're so hot, so wet," he said, and eased his body over hers between her thighs.

She wrapped her legs around his waist. He reached down between their bodies and positioned himself. Their gazes met and locked as he slowly entered her, inch by inch. When he could go no farther, he held himself still. She felt filled, stretched, and then he moved. Slowly, oh so slowly, he withdrew then thrust forward, again and again. She moved her hips, matching his rhythm. Pleasure began to coil inside her, deeper this time stronger, hotter.

"Chris, Chris." She called his name as her world exploded around her.

He stiffened, his jaw clenched and his hips moved faster and faster. She watched him through a veil of pleasure as he found his release. She held him, stroking his back until his body stopped shaking, and let her eyes drift closed. As his very essence surrounded her, she realized she felt more than attraction toward him, and that scared her.

They had to rush to arrive on time at Birmingham International Airport for their flight to Los Angeles. Renee was still reeling from awakening to Chris kissing his way down her body. She blushed, remembering how she'd screamed as he kissed and stroked her between her legs. She still couldn't get over the fact that she'd had three orgasms last night and one this morning. And to think, she hadn't enjoyed sex before. The few times she'd been with Marc had been rushed. Chris took his time.

Looking out the window of the rental car, Renee couldn't believe the sheer number of cars that were on the highway. She didn't like the traffic in Los Angeles. "Is it always like this?" she asked, staring at the long line of brake lights in front of them.

"Pretty much," he said. "Don't worry. We're almost there."

"I'm not worried. I'm just glad you're driving. I'll never complain about traffic in Birmingham again."

He laughed. "You get used to it and learn other ways around the city."

"Why did you leave?"

"Got a job with the bureau and I've been on the move ever since. I've lived in San Francisco, Dallas and now Atlanta."

"How can you move around so much? I'd hate to think about all that packing and unpacking."

"I don't have much to pack. Just a few boxes that I throw in the car and I'm ready to go."

"You've got to be kidding me," she said in horror. "I couldn't pack my hall with just a few boxes."

"I don't get attached to things. I keep important

papers, my clothes and my car. Other than that, I give away or sell everything else."

"How do you live like that? What about the things from your childhood?"

He laughed. "I don't have anything from my childhood. We were always one step away from being homeless. The few times we did have plenty of toys or clothes, something would happen and we'd end up leaving most of it behind. It's hard to skip out on rent if you're carrying a lot of stuff."

"So, now you don't keep anything?" she asked, her heart breaking for the boy and for the man who didn't realize what he was missing now.

"Nope." He exited the expressway. "Makes my life simple."

It also made it barren. He'd never really had a home, she realized. At least she'd had her parents' house and Aunt Gert's. He had no place.

A few minutes later, they entered the parking garage of Tyche International. The company was housed in a high-rise made of steel and glass. As they walked to the building, she smoothed the skirt of her black suit. Chris wanted her to look the part of a grieving widow like she'd done at the jewelry store. She couldn't grieve for Marc. The feelings she had for him were dead, but she could grieve for the life she'd hoped to have. A life that included a husband and the possibility of having children. Looking back, she wondered how she could have ever considered having children with Marc. He lacked qualities like honor, steadfastness and trust. Qualities his brother had in abundance.

Whoa. Where did that come from? She was *not* falling for Chris Foster. They would enjoy each other's company then go their separate ways. She pushed aside the doubt and walked into the building.

Bill Reynolds met them at the reception desk. He was a short, thin man with reddish-brown hair that was thinning on the top, and freckles.

"Mrs. Foster, I'm Bill Reynolds. I'm so sorry to meet you under these circumstances," he said, his sympathy for her clear in his tone.

"Thank you for meeting with us." Renee shook the man's hand. "I'm sorry I couldn't come out here sooner. Things have been so frantic since Marc died. This is Marc's brother, Chris Foster."

With a surprised look on his face, he turned to Chris. "Nice to meet you, too, Mr. Foster. If you'll follow me, I'll take you to Marc's office."

They walked down an aisle with light gray cubicles on either side. At the end of the aisle, they turned left. Marc's office was one of eight offices that had real walls. Reynolds took out a key and opened the dark panel door, which had an empty nameplate beside it. He opened the door and stepped inside. "I've already gone through and removed all the documents that were company related," he said, and motioned them inside.

Marc's office wasn't spacious, but it did have an excellent view of downtown. On his desk was a computer, a telephone and a cardboard box. Renee watched as Chris moved to the desk.

"Marc relied on you so much," Renee said to Mr. Reynolds. "He was in contact with you almost as much as he was with me."

"When you travel as much as the sales team does, you have to keep in constant contact or else they can end up someplace without the things they need," he said earnestly.

"And he appreciated you," Renee said. "He gave you his checkbook so you could handle things when he was overseas."

"Yes, and I've put it and the receipts in the box." He moved toward the door.

"Thank you," she said, then paused. "Chris, maybe Mr. Reynolds knows about the missing jewelry." She watched as the man's face turned red.

"Missing jewelry." He shook his head. "Don't know anything about that. Well, I'll be down the hall in my office if you need me. Take as much time as you need."

Chris waited until the man closed the door. "He's lying."

She nodded, agreeing with him one hundred percent. "What's in the box?"

He pulled back the flaps and opened the box. She walked to the desk and looked in. On top, in a silver frame, was a picture of a smiling woman and two boys.

She picked up the frame. "Is this your mother?"

He looked at the picture for a long time then replied, "Yes."

Renee held out the picture to him. "Marc looks a lot like her."

Slowly he took the frame. "Yeah, Marc favors Mom and I look like Dad. I didn't know he had this." He ran his fingers over his mother's face then set it on the desk.

He removed the rest of the contents of the box.

"Not much here," she said, looking at the calendar, blue silk tie, leather manicure kit and stack of framed certificates.

"No," he said, and began returning everything back to the box. "Reynolds knows something. I'm going to see if he'll talk to me alone. Maybe he doesn't feel comfortable talking in front of you if he knows about Marc's other wives."

"Fine with me."

He looked at the light signaling a message on the phone. "I also want to know if Marc has received any messages. I'm sure Reynolds or someone can check them."

"I'm surprised that one is there. Most companies take care of that pretty quickly when an employee leaves. I'd assume it's the same when one dies," she said.

He folded the flaps and closed the box. "I'll be back," he said and walked out the door.

She leaned back in the chair. If felt odd sitting in Marc's office, and sad. She looked at the box.

He'd worked here for four years and this was all that was left of him. He'd also left a legacy of lies and deception. She hoped Aunt Gert never learned about it. With nothing to do until Chris returned, she pulled out her PDA from her purse and played solitaire.

"Reynolds is going to meet with me at six tonight," he said when he returned.

She looked at her watch. It was 9:45 a.m. "What do we do until then?"

He picked up the box. "We've got plenty of time before we check in to the hotel. I can show you Los Angeles and take you to one of the best Korean restaurants in town."

"Sounds like a plan to me."

He took her to all the touristy places she wanted to go. Near the corner of Hollywood and Highland, he parked the car and waited patiently as she took pictures of the hillside with the famous Hollywood sign. He walked with her down the street to Mann's Chinese Theater where she took more pictures and asked another tourist to take their picture in front of the crowded theater. She could tell he was humoring her, but she didn't care. He laughed with her as she tried to find a footprint that fit her shoes.

"You know, you can buy postcards with better pictures," he said as he looked over his shoulder at the viewing screen on her digital camera.

"They wouldn't be my pictures," she said with a

smile, "but I am going to buy some postcards. Let's find Hattie McDaniel's star. I want to take a picture for Aunt Gert."

They found the star and he took a picture of her kneeling beside it, then insisted they eat lunch. He took her hand as they walked back to the car. She told herself that it was no big deal, but in fact it was. He was the first man other than her father to hold her hand. As they walked down the street, she knew that this moment would be the one she remembered most.

Later, he drove away from the tourist attractions and into an area of town where most of the signs were in a foreign language. He parked in front of a small strip mall and led her to the restaurant. The lunch crowd had filled almost all of the tables. Everywhere she looked, signs were in Korean, and listening to the conversations around, which she assumed were in Korean, she wondered how he'd found the place. She was about to ask him, when a woman with thick gray hair and Asian features came forward speaking rapidly.

Renee understood "Mr. Chris" but that was all. The woman led them to a table and hurried away.

"How did you find this place?" Renee asked.

"The owners invited Will and me here when we responded to a call. We started coming here when we wanted great barbecue."

"Who's Will?" she asked.

"Will Johnson is a friend and my old partner when I was on the police force here."

"Does he still live here?" she asked as the waiter placed a teapot and cups on the table.

"Oh, yeah, Will has family here. As a matter of fact, he said he'd try to meet us here for lunch."

Minutes later, the waiter brought a large tray filled with bowls of food to their table. She looked at the amount of food on the table and said, "We'll need help eating all of this. Why did you order so much?"

"I ordered barbecue. Mrs. Koh sent the rest."

She added a little of everything onto her plate then took her first bite of barbecue. "Oh, this is good," she said.

"The lady has excellent taste." A tall man with light brown skin and black hair walked to the table. Chris stood and shook hands with him.

"Will, this is Renee Foster."

"Nice to meet you," he said. Will looked down at the table of food then at Chris. "Mrs. Koh did this."

Chris nodded and Will sat in the chair beside him.

"Why would Mrs. Koh send over all this food?" Renee asked, watching Will pile food on his plate.

"She thinks we're some kind of heroes because we stopped them from getting robbed a few years ago. Since then, she and her husband have been trying to feed us." Will began eating.

She looked at Chris. "You seem to have a knack for stopping robberies."

"No, I don't. I just do my job," Chris said.

She gave him a skeptical look. Will laughed. "Chris is modest. I'm not. I'll tell you that I'm plain wonderful."

"So you keep saying. Maybe one day somebody will believe you," Chris said drily.

Renee listened and watched as the two men interacted. It was plain to see they were good friends. During the middle of lunch, Will's cell phone rang and he had to leave.

Shortly afterward, they left. When Chris tried to pay the bill, Mrs. Koh refused to take his money.

They drove across town to a small park. Strolling along the walkway, she stopped to admire the rose garden and read the signs describing the types of roses. "I think these will grow in my garden," she said.

"I have no clue," he said.

"You're no help." She glanced longingly at the orange roses.

"Nope." He took her hand and continued down the walkway past a few tables set on the lawn.

"Mathematical Association," he said, reading the poster on one of the tables. "That's up your alley."

She looked at the displays encouraging mathematical study. They stopped to watch a minimath competition between two high school math teams.

"I think I understood half of what they were talking about," he said as they walked away.

"Don't worry. There isn't a quiz later," she said.

He laughed and they walked to the last display that consisted of the statement "Solve this problem." An older man sat behind the table, watching as two people wrote on sheets of paper. Renee looked at the problem for a minute. It didn't look so bad. If she'd been alone, she would have attempted to solve it, but she wasn't comfortable doing it with Chris there. He knew she was smart, but it was something else to witness it. A group of college students wandered to the table.

"I'm telling you. Nobody's going to solve it and it sure won't be a girl," a lanky young man with long brown hair said.

"You're so full of it, Eric," a young woman with short blond hair spat back.

"If you're so sure, pony up. A hundred dollars says a girl won't solve that problem."

"I'll take that bet." The young lady held out her hand.

Renee wanted to compete now more than ever, but the day was going so well and she didn't want to do anything to spoil it. Her intelligence intimidated most men.

Chris turned to her. "Are you going to prove that idiot wrong?"

"I hadn't planned on it," she said.

"Go ahead. Do your thing. It will be good for the rest of the girls here."

Renee couldn't believe what she was hearing. He wanted her to show off her intelligence in public? "Are you sure you don't mind?"

He shrugged. "Why would I mind? Show everyone the real Renee."

She looked at him and at that moment realized that she'd fallen in love with him.

Chapter 11

That night, Renee waited in her hotel room for Chris to return from his meeting with Bill Reynolds. It had been too late to cancel one room so they'd kept both. She sat on her bed and tried to come to grips with the fact that she loved Chris Foster. She would never tell him. The people she loved would always leave her; her parents, even Marc, whom she hadn't loved but wanted to love, had left her. Aunt Gert was the exception.

Chris would leave her without a doubt. He was already making plans to move from Atlanta to Washington, D.C. She'd have to keep her feelings to herself.

Her heart raced when she heard the locks disengage. He walked into the room with a folder in his hand and smiled. "I really like seeing you in the middle of the bed."

"There's plenty of room." She patted the side closest to him. "Join me."

He shook his head. "Unfortunately you and I have places to be." He walked to one of the lounge chairs and sat down. "Reynolds bought several pieces of jewelry from a place called La Luna. That's where we're heading."

She looked down at her black pants. "Do I need to change into the suit?"

"No. It won't matter," he said.

La Luna was located in a new building that had been designed and decorated to look old and was a combination art gallery and jewelry store. There were plenty of customers wandering around the two-story building.

A tall woman with short, black hair and pale skin greeted them. "Welcome to La Luna. How can I help you?"

Chris flashed his badge and introduced himself. "Can you tell us if anyone came in here looking for information about this necklace or how they could sell it?" Chris showed her a picture of Miss Gert's necklace.

The lady studied the necklace for a few seconds. "Yes. A customer wanted to know if someone could design something similar to this. Talk to Edmond. He can tell you more."

Renee felt a kick of excitement. Would they finally find it? She hoped so. The lady led them to Edmond, who was an older man with age spots and a sharp eye. He remembered the necklace. "Yes. A guy came in a few months ago and wanted to know the names of designers who could make this necklace."

"Did you give him names?" Chris asked.

"I gave him two names. Both designers use this art deco style in their work. Like this ring." He pointed to a ring in the display case. "Do you want the names of the designers?"

"Yes," he said.

"Alfred Belmont is one. He's here in California. We carried a few of his pieces before he became big. The other designer is in New York—her name is Arella. Does good work."

"Would either of them buy a necklace like this?" Renee asked.

"Alfred could afford to buy it, but I don't think Arella could," Edmond said.

"Do you have a number or address where I can reach either of them?" Chris added.

"I'll get them." The old man walked away.

Renee waited until he was out of sight. "Why would Marc want designers?"

"Designers know how to redesign stolen jewelry or they might know who's interested in buying stolen jewelry," Chris said.

The thought of Aunt Gert's necklace being taken apart gave her a sick feeling in her stomach. Instead of thinking about that possibility, Renee studied the jewelry inside the display case. The ring Edmond had pointed out was beautiful. The cocktail ring had a large princess-cut diamond in the center with smaller diamonds surrounding it. Its style reminded her of Aunt Gert's necklace.

Edmond returned and gave Chris a piece of paper. "Here's the information. I hope you find what you're looking for."

"Thanks," Chris replied.

"I'd like to see the ring," Renee said when the men shook hands.

Edmond smiled and unlocked the case. The ring was a little loose on her finger but it looked gorgeous. She listened with half an ear to Edmond's description of the ring. "Who designed this ring?" she asked, admiring the way it looked on her hand.

"Arella designed it," he said.

She wanted it and winced when Edmond told her the cost. Reluctantly she returned the ring. "I'd like your card. I can't buy the ring now, but if it's still here later, I want it," she told him.

"Absolutely." He gave her his card.

Chris remained silent during the exchange but gave Edmond his card, also. The older man's eyebrows lifted when he read the card. They left the store and drove toward the hotel.

"Are you hungry?" Chris asked.

"No. I'm still full from lunch," she said as she looked over the file Bill Reynolds had given

Chris. "Marc bought a lot of jewelry, but none of the wives received much. I wonder what he did with it all?"

"Tell Danielle and Alex to check Marc's clothing. He might have hidden some of it there."

Renee reached into her purse. "You're right," she said as she dialed Danielle's number. "I can't help but think he has them someplace else. Hey, Danielle. It's Renee."

"Hello, Renee. How's it going?" Her voice was as smooth and sensual as her looks.

"Good. Listen, you need to search Marc's clothes. He bought a lot of jewelry. More than I think he ever gave us, and Chris thinks some of it might be hidden in his clothes."

"What! That lying ass," Danielle said coldly.

"Yeah. I know. Chris found a gold credit card and a Florida license in one of Marc's jackets at my house."

"If he weren't already dead..." she muttered.

"I know," Renee said.

"Hey, did you find your aunt's necklace?"

"No, but we're still looking. We're in Los Angeles now. We went to Marc's job to pick up his things."

Danielle sighed. "One day, we'll look back and wonder how we made it through this. On a happier note, have you decided what to wear to Alex's wedding?"

"No. I'd planned to buy something when I got home."

"How long are you going to be in L.A.?" Danielle asked.

"We're leaving early tomorrow."

"Stop by my friend's shop, Cocoa. She sells beautiful clothes, and I'm sure she'll have something that's perfect for the wedding. Tell her I sent you."

"Okay, I'll stop by." Renee heard static on the line. "I'd better call Alex before I totally lose my cell phone signal."

"Do you want me to call Alex? I've got to call her anyway and I'll tell her to check Marc's clothes."

"Sure. Thank you, Danielle." Renee ended the call. "Danielle's going to call Alex," she told him.

"Good. If you're not hungry, then I'll grab a sandwich before we get back to the hotel."

"Go ahead, but do you think we can find a place called Cocoa? Danielle thinks I should go there to look for a dress for Alex's wedding."

Hours later, they returned to the hotel. "I can't believe I let you talk me into buying those clothes." Renee dropped her bags on the bed.

He put the bags he carried on the bed beside hers. "They look good on you."

He'd made her model the outfits. He and Danielle's friend, Cocoa, had critiqued them with brutal honesty. They found the perfect lavender silk dress for her to wear to the wedding. "I don't know if they'll all fit in my suitcase."

"Put some of them in mine," he said, loosening his tie.

There was a certain intimacy in placing your clothes in another's suitcase. When she finished packing, she climbed on the bed where Chris studied the notes and receipts Bill Reynolds gave him.

"Marc made a lot of trips to New York and California on commercial flights," he said.

"He could have easily met with either jewelry designer," she said, wishing she'd brought her laptop with her. She'd have to wait until she got home before she could do research on them.

Chris closed the file and put it on the nightstand. "There's something I've been wanting to do all day," he said and gathered her into his arms.

"What have you wanted to do all day?" she asked in a teasing voice.

"This," he said, and kissed her, long, slow and softly.

"Scratch Alfred Belmont off the list," Chris said, closing his cell phone. "There's a nine-month wait before he'll consult with new clients." They'd arrived in Birmingham a few hours ago and began gathering research on the two designers immediately.

He sat at "his" desk, searching for information on Belmont while Renee searched for information on Arella. He stretched his arms, attempting to work the stiffness out of his shoulders from sitting at his computer.

Watching Renee work was always interesting. She wore a turquoise dress he'd convinced her to buy in Los Angeles. The dress showed off her curvy figure.

"I'm not coming up with much on Arella," she said. "I'm still looking. The phone number is good, but no answer so far."

"If it's a cell phone, it might not get a good signal."

"That's true. I'm going to stop looking for information on her for a while. There's something bothering me about Marc's finances. I know he juggled money around, but I'm going to look there for a while."

"Okay. I'll search for Arella. I'm getting coffee. Do you want more?"

"Yes, and bring some cookies. I'm hungry."

He went to the kitchen and poured two cups of coffee—black for him and light and sweet for her. They were as different as their tastes in coffee. He never settled down in one place and she'd planted roots deep in the Alabama soil. Yet, he wanted her and craved her company. For now, he'd enjoy his time with her because in a week he'd be back in Atlanta. He piled a bunch of cookies on a plate and balanced the two cups of coffee in his hand. Don't think about the future, he told himself.

When he walked into the office, she was standing beside his desk and frowning. *When had that become his desk?*

"What's wrong?" He put down the cups and held out the plate of cookies.

She selected one and said with disgust, "Marc used three different social security numbers."

"Really?"

"Yeah." Renee bit hard into the cookie.

"Talk to your lawyer," he said.

"Oh, I plan to…believe me…and then I'm…"

The sound of the doorbell stopped her.

She marched to the door. Chris wanted to throw something. What else could Marc do wrong?

"Guess who's coming home tonight, or this morning, rather?" Terrell Smithstone entered the foyer wearing shorts, a T-shirt and flip-flops, looking nothing like the hard-nosed attorney he'd dealt with a few weeks ago.

"Who?" Renee asked.

"Karen. She's finished and we're having a party. Mom wants you to bake something Karen would like. And bring Miss Gert." He stopped and looked at her. "You look nice."

"Thanks. I'll be there. Why didn't she tell anybody so we could plan?"

"She wasn't sure she'd finish this soon. Anyway, gotta run. Oh, bring him with you," Smithstone said.

"Wait. I need to talk to you as my lawyer," Renee said.

"What?" Smithstone gave Chris a hard look.

"Marc used three different social security numbers. I need you to tell me how to minimize the damage," Renee said.

Chris admired Smithstone's ability to control his anger. "I'll tell you what I find out. Don't worry."

"I'll try anyway. And please tell your mom I'm making chocolate cake."

"Bake two. You know between Dad and Karen, there won't be any cake left for the rest of us…and come early." He turned to Chris. "Foster, fair warning. Hang with the guys tomorrow."

"I'll keep that in mind," he said.

"See y'all tomorrow," Smithstone said and left.

Chris looked at her. "Are your cakes as good as your cookies?"

"I think my cakes are better."

"Maybe you should make three cakes."

She laughed. "I'll make three cakes if you keep me company in the kitchen."

"You've got a deal." He went to the office and retrieved his laptop and some files. If his being in the kitchen with her made her happy then he was there.

She began gathering ingredients and placing them on the counter.

"How long has your friend been out of town?" He put the laptop on the small table.

"Over a year. She was in South Africa." She removed eggs, butter and milk from the refrigerator and set them on the counter.

"Beautiful country."

She looked at him in surprise. "You've been there? I wanted to visit her but I never got the chance."

He'd bet Marc was the reason she hadn't gone to see her friend. "Once to Cape Town. I'd go there again. What was she doing in South Africa?"

"Working. She's a psychiatrist."

"Speaking of work, I'd better get at it," he said. "I want to check a few things before the baseball game starts. Do you like baseball?"

"I can take it or leave it. I'm more of a football fan."

"Do you mind if I watch the game tonight? The Braves are playing."

"No. The television's all yours tonight."

He opened a file folder and looked at the photograph of a younger Miss Gert. "Miss Gert likes jewelry. Do you know what happened to the earrings that matched the necklace?"

"I don't know. You'll have to ask her about them," Renee said and began mixing.

"You don't wear a lot of jewelry."

"No, but I love jewelry. I haven't bought a lot of it. I'm going to change that."

"You should. You like books and you buy those."

She smiled at him. "You're right. I like Aunt Gert's necklace, but I'd never buy something like that for me. I like something less flashy for a necklace. Now a ring is different."

"I'm afraid to ask, but why is a ring different?"

"Well, it's smaller, more discreet and you can get

away with wearing a flashy ring with plain clothes more than a flashy necklace." Her smile was mysterious.

"Is this a woman thing that no man can possibly ever understand?"

"Yes."

He shook his head and started working. It surprised him how comfortable he was with her. He liked talking with her. It wouldn't take much to get used to having her around, and that worried him.

Chapter 12

The Smithstones lived two houses down from Renee. Chris had picked up Aunt Gert an hour ago and the three of them carried one cake each as they walked down the sidewalk to the party. She felt feminine wearing the peach shorts and a matching floral tank top that she'd bought in Los Angeles.

"I can't wait to see Karen," Aunt Gert said. "The pictures she e-mailed to us were lovely."

"I'm sure Karen's ready to see you, too," Renee said, eager to see her friend. Calls, e-mails and instant messaging weren't the same as a visit.

She looked over her shoulder to check on Chris. He looked good in tan shorts and a white polo shirt.

In addition to the cake, he also carried two folding lounge chairs. He met her gaze and smiled at her. Her pulse fluttered. Being with him made her realize how much she'd missed by settling with Marc.

Never again.

Chris made her feel wanted and desired. He made her desire things she'd long ago given up on.

They walked up the front walkway and around to the back. Renee opened the gate to the backyard. A large patio stretched along the entire back of the house. At the far end, Karen and Terrell's father, Mr. Smithstone, manned his enormous stainless-steel grill that billowed smoke and tantalizing aromas. Three folding tables were covered with a variety of covered dishes and paraphernalia.

Mr. Smithstone smiled when he saw them. "Set those down before Karen comes out," he said, motioning to one of the tables.

They put the cakes on the table. Renee's mouth began to water. "Where is she?" Renee asked.

At that moment, Karen opened the glass patio door and squealed. Delighted, Renee ran across the wooden deck and hugged her.

Karen returned the hug then stepped back. "Look at you. I love the outfit. I missed you. Tell me everything."

Renee laughed. "You haven't changed a bit."

"Of course she hasn't," Aunt Gert interrupted and hugged Karen.

Karen looked at Chris and smiled. "You must be Chris. My brother said you were here." She held out her hand.

"Nice to meet you," Chris said and shook her hand.

"Daddy, tell him where you want the chairs," Karen said and looped her arm through Renee's.

When Chris and Aunt Gert walked over to talk to Mr. Smithstone, Karen whispered, "He's handsome. Terrell said he was pretty nice. Is he?"

"One of the nicest men I know," Renee said.

"You'll have to fill me in later. I know we won't get to talk much today. I promise we will soon."

Renee hugged her again. "I missed you." Now that Karen was back, she realized how much she'd come to rely on her bubbly but down-to-earth view of the world.

"Is there something wrong?" her friend asked.

She longed to tell her everything, but she couldn't. Instead she shook her head. "No. I'm just glad you're back."

Friends and neighbors began arriving with more food and greetings. Within minutes, the patio was abuzz with activity and Karen was the queen bee. Renee saw Chris talking with Terrell and a group of neighbors. Seeing him stand there somehow looked right. It was as if this was where he was supposed to be. She pushed the thought aside. Chris turned, met her gaze. She was beginning to get used to the way he made her heart jump. She watched as he stepped away from the group of men and walked to her. He looked at her like she was the only person he wanted to be with.

"Some party," he said when he reached her.

"Yes. It is. Are you having fun?"

"I am. Let's grab those chairs." He pointed to two empty seats in the midst of a group of friends talking. Soon, they were enveloped in three separate conversations. As time passed, Renee realized that this was the kind of life she wanted. Surrounded by friends, family and acceptance. When she looked at Chris her heart melted and she thought of the possibility of having this life.

From the kitchen window, Karen and Miss Gert watched Renee and Chris.

"What do you make of him?" the older woman asked.

Karen studied Chris for a few seconds then looked at Renee's relaxed smile. "I think he makes her happy."

Miss Gert nodded. Whatever it was that had worried Renee for the last few weeks seemed to be gone. "Yes. I believe you're right."

"She's worried about something. I could see it in her face earlier."

"I know. She won't tell me about it."

"Is it Marc?" Karen asked.

"I don't believe it is. I know she cared for Marc, but she didn't love him. There's a certain air around a couple in love and they didn't have it." She studied the couple outside. They didn't have the air of love around them either, but there was something. "We'll have to keep an eye on them."

Karen agreed.

Hours later, Renee sipped on a can of ginger ale as she sat listening to Chris and Karen debate the merits of Kenyan coffee, Karen's favorite, versus Chris's favorite, Columbian coffee.

"Renee."

She sat up straight at the sound of her mother's voice. She turned around to see her parents standing a few yards away from her. Unlike the rest of the people at the party, who wore shorts and casual clothing, her parents were dressed as if they were headed to Sunday morning church service.

"Hi. I didn't know you were in town," she said, shocked to see them, then felt her stomach burn at the annoyed and disapproving look on both of their faces.

"We called when we got to the airport, but you obviously weren't answering either of your phones. Why have two phones if you're not going to answer either of them? That is irresponsible, Renee," her father said stiffly.

Embarrassed, she said, "I'm sorry."

Chris looked at Renee's parents. She had her father's features and he wondered why they were so angry with her for missing their call.

"You could have called her sooner. Given her

some advanced notice that you were coming to town." Miss Gert's tone was calm, but he could hear the anger beneath it.

"We gave her plenty of notice this afternoon," her mother said.

Chris heard Karen mutter a cuss.

"Renee is here to celebrate my return home. Since you're here, why don't you join us and enjoy Renee's company here?" Karen said.

Her father stiffened as if she'd insulted him. "We can't possibly stay. We have a two-hour layover until we fly to Chicago. Renee, we need to discuss an opportunity for you."

He'd had enough of these people. "I'm sorry. We haven't met. I'm Chris Foster, Marc's younger brother." He held out his hand and stepped between Renee and her parents.

Her father shook his hand reluctantly. "James and Lorna Mitchell. I'm sorry, but we really need to speak with our daughter."

"You should have thought of that before showing up on her doorstep unannounced. She'd made plans that didn't include you. Next time, have the common decency to respect her and her time."

"Chris," Renee said. "It's okay. I…"

He looked at her. Her face was flushed with embarrassment. "No. It's not okay. They are treating you with disrespect and I won't have that."

"You can't tell us how to treat our own daughter," her mother said sharply.

"I just did," he said softly.

Her mother looked at Renee. "Why are you treating us like this? We love you."

Miss Gert rose out of her chair. "Lorna. You stop badgering her and either get a plate or hit the road."

She glared at the older woman then turned to Renee. "When you've come to your senses, give us a call." She turned, took her husband's arm and they walked away.

"Wait," Renee called after them.

Chris put his hand on her shoulder. "Let them go. They were wrong to treat you that way."

"But…"

"He's right," Karen said. "They've been emotionally abusive to you for a long time. What they are doing to you isn't out of love."

Karen put her arms around Renee's shoulders and led her to the chair. Flanked by Karen and Miss Gert, he saw her wipe away tears. Anger flowed through him as he watched her. What kind of parents were those people?

Terrell caught his gaze and motioned him away from the women. They walked to the other side of the yard. Chris stood where he could keep an eye on Renee.

"What's the story with her parents?" he asked.

Terrell looked at him. "Renee's parents are the kind of people who should never have children. They treat her like crap and expect her to jump whenever they say jump."

Terrell's father joined them. "Thank you for telling them off. I've wanted to do it for years."

"If they didn't want Renee, why didn't they let Miss Gert raise her?" Chris asked.

"That would be bad for their image and too much like right," Mr. Smithstone said. "Miss Gert wanted to raise Renee, but those two enjoyed being the parents of a genius without doing the work of being parents. They say they love her, but they don't know what love is. It takes a lot of real love and work to raise a genius." He put his arm around his son. "Isn't that right, boy genius?"

"What are you talking about? I was the perfect child," Terrell said and put his arm around his father's shoulder.

"In your dreams," the older man said.

Chris watched as the women gathered around Renee to give her comfort. He now understood why she'd married Marc. Her relationship with her parents had given her a very skewed view of love. She was still trying to get her parents to learn to love her. She deserved more. She deserved more than he could give her.

"She deserves love." Chris hadn't meant to say the words aloud.

"Yes. She deserves it," Terrell said. "She has our love and she always will."

Chris watched her and wondered what he could do to ease her pain.

* * *

Later that evening, Chris walked home with Renee. Terrell drove Miss Gert to her condo, which was not far from his town house. Renee had been more subdued since her parents departure.

"I like your friends," he said when they entered the kitchen.

"You mean Karen's friends," she said, locking the door.

"No. I mean your friends, the Smithstones and your neighbors. They're all your friends. I had a really good time with them."

"Even when my parents came?" she asked with sadness in her brown eyes.

"Even then," he said, and put his arms around her shoulders.

"I wish you hadn't talked to them that way. I know you were trying to help. I try so hard to be the daughter they want me to be, but I keep messing up."

He took her hand and led her out of the kitchen to the sofa in the den. He sat down beside her. "You are not your parents' problem. They are the problem. You are a wonderful person, Renee."

She tried to smile but her lips trembled. "Now you sound like Karen."

"She's a professional. You should listen to her."

He watched, feeling helpless as tears rolled down her cheeks. "They don't love me. They've never loved me," she said softly and with dead certainty. She looked into his eyes. "What's wrong with me?"

His heart felt as if it had been squeezed. He wrapped his arms around her and pulled her close. "There's nothing wrong with you. Absolutely nothing." He rocked her in his arms and stroked her hair as she cried.

Later, her tears spent, she tilted her head back and looked up at him. Brushing his thumb across her cheek, he thought she looked so beautiful. He lowered his lips to her forehead and kissed her softly, ignoring the slow curl of desire he felt. She needed tenderness, not lust, he told himself. He leaned back, studying her face, enjoying the sight of her.

She lifted her hand and with gentle fingers traced his top lip then his bottom. Desire made him tremble and he couldn't get enough air. He parted his lips and she slipped the tip of her finger inside his mouth. Without thinking, he sucked.

Heat flashed into her eyes. She withdrew her finger, pressed forward and kissed him. Her tongue slipped between his lips, past his teeth. In and out, she thrust her tongue into his mouth in a familiar mating dance. He stroked her back, feeling a shudder run through her body. The feel of her soft breasts against his chest made his skin burn. Desire, which he'd tried to contain, burst free when she stroked his chest.

She freed her lips and kissed his chin, his jaw and his neck, sending his body into full-alert. He threaded his fingers through her hair. "Look at me," he said, his voice raspy.

She looked at him; desire was there in her gaze, but there was also a hint of uncertainty and vulnerability. He knew she didn't need his tenderness right now. She needed to know beyond a shadow of a doubt that she was wanted, needed and desired. He planned to show her in vivid detail that he wanted, needed and above all desired only her.

He lowered his head. Using both hands, he held her face and poured everything he had into his kiss. He used his tongue, teeth and lips. Licking, sucking, biting. Feasting on her mouth until her shoulders shook hard with passion.

He lifted his mouth and reveled in the sound of her harsh breathing. He positioned her until she was sitting with her shoulders against the back of sofa. Reaching out, he teased her nipple with the tip of his finger. Her back straightened and she leaned into his touch. Giving her one last featherlight stroke on her nipple, he peeled down the straps of her top and bra, revealing her lush, brown flesh. Fisting his hands, he fought the need to push her down on the couch and ravish her. Reaching behind her with shaking hands, he unfastened her clasp and helped free her arms from the straps of her clothes.

She took his hand and pressed it to her breast, her hard nipple pressed against his palm. Suddenly it wasn't enough. He wanted his mouth on her, his hands touching her everywhere. He felt his control slipping. A heartbeat later, he was on his knees in front of her, pushing her legs apart to make room for him. Lowering his head, he kissed her breast then cupped it and licked her nipple as if it were a chocolate ice cream cone on a hot summer's day. He heard her moans and felt the bite of her nails on his shoulder. Turning his head, he nuzzled her other breast and took her nipple into his mouth. He suckled, wrapped his arms around her waist and urged her closer to him. He released her from his lips, sat back on his haunches and let his gaze drink in the sight of her. She looked passionate, tempting and wantonly hot.

Chris reached out and rubbed his hand along her inner thigh. Slipping his hand inside the hem of her loose shorts, he pushed the fabric higher and higher until he could feel her damp heat through her thin panties. She moved her hips against his fingers and he moaned. Slowly he withdrew and moved to the waistband of her shorts. Rising to his knees, his hands trembled as he pulled the snap then pulled down the zipper. Sliding his fingers over her top and inside the waistband of her shorts and panties, he sat on his haunches and slowly pulled. She gripped his shoulders and lifted her hips and he slid her clothes off her hips, exposing the black triangle of curls between her legs. Moving back, he pulled her clothes down her legs and over her sandals.

Groaning, he moved between her legs, spreading them wide. Sliding his hands up her thighs, he leaned down and kissed the side of her knee. He traveled up, kissing the warm skin of her inner thigh, higher and higher, breathing deep to smell her sweet perfume. He gently bit her inner thigh. Her legs clenched and her hips arched forward. His heart hammered against the walls of his chest. He slid his finger inside her hot, slick core and moved. In and out. He put another finger inside her, loving the wild groans coming from her lips. When he couldn't hold out any longer, he removed his fingers from inside her, spread her, then kissed and licked her womanly core. He devoured her until she screamed his name.

Later that night, Renee awakened alone in her bed. She shivered as she remembered the things Chris had done to her on the sofa and later here in her bed. He'd given her pleasure like she'd never known and her body was still humming. Glancing at her nightstand, she noted the time. It was nearly two o'clock in the morning. Through the open doors, she saw a faint light coming from downstairs.

What was he doing up so late?

She walked naked to her bathroom and grabbed her robe. She followed the light downstairs to the office.

Chris sat at the desk with his laptop opened in front of him. Shirtless, he looked deliciously naked. Everything that made her a woman responded to his masculine grace and power. The love she felt for him filled her heart and overflowed. It scared her at times, but right now, it comforted her. She walked inside and he smiled at her.

"What are you doing?" She stopped beside the desk, a little disappointed to see that he wore white boxers. Another day, maybe she could talk him into working naked.

"I'm trying to get into Marc's hard drive without destroying all the data," he said.

It was then that she noticed the small, silver hard drive beside his laptop.

"This isn't the hard drive that I gave him. Are you sure this belongs to Marc?"

He rubbed the back of neck. "It was found in Marc's plane."

She stepped away from the desk. Shocked, angry and hurt by his omission. "What? Why didn't you tell me? What else are you keeping from me?"

He leaned back in his chair. "Keeping from you?"

Folding her arms across her chest, she frowned at him. "I had the right to know about it. It might have the location of Aunt Gert's necklace."

"Or it could have information on Alex or Danielle that has nothing to do with you. I don't share personal information about you to them or vice versa," he said in a low, cool tone.

"Wait a minute. This isn't about personal information. This is about the truth. You haven't told any of the wives about it, have you?"

"No, and until I know what's on the hard drive, I hope you won't tell Alex or Danielle about it."

She stared at him. "Do you have any idea how arrogant and deceitful that statement is?"

He folded his arms across his chest. "No. Why don't you explain it to me, Renee."

She clenched her jaw, so angry with him she could spit. "All right. I will. Marc has either flat-out lied or lied by omission on so many things that I, no, all three wives are trying to figure out what's real and what's not." She put her hands on her hips and continued. "Then here you come, Mr. FBI-Y chromosome, making executive decisions about who should know what and when. Let me just tell you something. You don't have the *right* to keep information from us. We have been through *heck* because of him. And I don't give a skinny rat's patootie if there's not a thing on that drive that pertains to me, but I still have the right to know it exists. Is that clear enough for ya?"

He said nothing for a few seconds then said, "I understand."

"Good. And another thing. If you'd said something sooner, I could have…" She stopped then turned away. What was she doing? "Never mind."

"You could have what?"

She bit her lip. She'd said too much. Now, she would have to tell him. With resignation, she realized she would have had to tell a portion of the story anyway. When she looked up, she met his dark, probing gaze and wondered just how much to tell him.

"If you'd told me about the hard drive sooner, I could have given you everything on it."

He unfolded his arms, leaned forward. His pale brown eyes focused solely on her. "How?"

Renee decided to tell him the whole truth. "You know Calvin Gaines."

"Yeah. He owns the biggest computer security company in the world. His company does a lot of work for the government. Do you know him?"

She nodded.

"Will you ask him to get into Marc's hard drive?"

"I don't have to. I can do it," she said softly.

"You can do it," he repeated. "How do you know Calvin Gaines?"

"We attended Duke University and we took a few computer science classes together. In one of the classes, we had a group project to study the strengths and weaknesses of network security in big companies or organizations. Well, the thing is—" She stopped to gather her nerve. "We got into the network of the North Carolina State Bureau of Investigation."

He sat back in his chair. "Aw, man."

"We didn't delete files or do anything malicious," she said quickly.

"They found out, didn't they?"

"Cal and I were questioned by the FBI and SBI. It was scary."

"How old were the two of you?"

"I was sixteen. I think Cal was seventeen. I tried

to explain the class project to them, but they didn't care. I had to show them how I got on their network. After that, I changed my major from computer science to mathematics. It was safer."

Chris shook his head. "Tell me you're not a hacker now."

She shrugged her shoulders. "I only hack into Cal's stuff."

He looked at her for a long moment then picked up the hard drive and gave it to her. "See what you can do with this."

Twenty minutes later, she'd gotten past all the safeguards and encryption codes on the hard drive and accessed the files. She felt a punch of excitement when she read the first file. "Chris. You need to see this."

He rolled his chair next to hers and looked at the computer. Two photographs were on the computer screen. The first was of Aunt Gert wearing the necklace and earrings with the caption Gertrude Alma Lee Mitchell (GMALNL) below it. The second photograph was the necklace and earrings in a black display case with the caption Arella Laveau (ALNYER).

He pointed to the captions. "That's what was written in Marc's organizer."

She nodded, remembering the entry. She scrolled down the file and spotted an address. "There's Arella's address."

Chapter 13

Getting in touch with Arella Laveau had been harder than either of them had expected. Two days later, while driving to Atlanta to attend Alex and Hunter's wedding, Chris received a phone call from the designer.

"She's agreed to meet with us when she returns to New York tomorrow," he said, closing his cell phone.

Renee sat in the passenger seat of his Explorer, ignoring the fast-moving traffic and skyscrapers of downtown Atlanta. She'd listened to Chris's end of the conversation with an anxious knot in her stomach. She was sure Laveau had Aunt Gert's necklace but the brief exchange told her nothing. "Why didn't you ask her about the necklace?" she asked.

Chris put his cell phone on the console between the seats and put his hand on the wheel. "We could barely hear each other through the static." He looked at her then moved his hand over the console and covered hers. "Don't worry. We'll talk to her tomorrow. Relax."

His hand felt warm, comfortable and strong. She turned her hand and twined her fingers with his. The knot in her stomach loosened a little. "We still have to get plane tickets to New York."

"We'll get tickets. For now, we've got a wedding to attend. Hunter and Alex deserve our attention now," he said.

She considered his statement. "I'll try not to think about it when we get to the yacht, but until then I need to think about it now." She squeezed his hand and sighed. "It's so frustrating. I wish you'd asked her about the necklace."

He shook his head. "She wouldn't have told us anything over the phone. Anyone who's in her business is very careful. No one wants to be robbed or killed."

She hadn't considered the possible danger to the designer. After her experience in H. Morgan and Sons Jewelers, she couldn't blame the woman for being careful. "You're right. I should relax and focus on the wedding because there's nothing I can do about the necklace now."

"We'll be at the hotel in a few minutes. I'm sure

Alex and Danielle will keep us busy for the rest of the day," he said.

"Why do you say that?" she asked, enjoying the simple act of holding his hand.

"Hunter filled me in when I called him last night. They're keeping the wedding arrangements as quiet as possible."

"I can't imagine living my life like Alex and Danielle. Every time they go out, they have to be prepared to have their picture taken." She shuddered. "I wouldn't do that."

"No, you'd rather give your attention to those you love than have the attention be on you. You're a generous woman." He lifted their joined hands and kissed her fingers.

She smiled at him then turned her head to stare blindly out of the passenger window. Her heart ached. He'd come to know her well in a short period of time. He'd also managed to capture her heart totally and completely. It still amazed her how quickly he cut through all of her defenses and how he'd settle for nothing less than the real her. She wanted him to stay with her so badly that it scared her.

"We're here," he said, bringing the car to a stop beneath the covered entrance of the hotel.

They quickly checked in to their adjoining rooms and changed clothes. Danielle and Tristan were waiting in the lobby. Danielle wore a pink silk wrap dress that hugged her curves without being overly suggestive. She looked glamorous, feminine and gorgeous. She smiled and hurried over to Renee and Chris when she saw them step out of the elevator.

"Renee, you look great. Cocoa told me that you'd found a wonderful dress for the wedding." Danielle gave her a hug, then stepped back and circled Renee to get a good look at the dress.

"Thanks to you. I'd never have gone there if you hadn't suggested it, and you look wonderful yourself," Renee replied.

"Thank you," Danielle said and smiled at Chris when he stood beside her.

"Hello, Danielle. Tristan," he said as Tristan joined Danielle.

"Hello," Tristan said, then added, "Our ride is here."

The driver of the 1930's white limousine held the door open for them. Renee felt like a princess as she climbed inside. The ride to the marina was short. They walked down the pier to the Marc III. From there, a young man dressed in a black suit led them to the upper deck.

Hunter stood in the rear, talking to an older man. He ended the conversation with the man and walked toward the group.

"What a lovely day for a wedding," Danielle said.

Hunter smiled in agreement. It was an unusually mild day with temperatures in the midseventies. "Yes, it is. Now that everyone is here we can get started," he said.

"Anxious," Chris said and smiled.

Hunter smiled, then said, "Yes." He led them inside a small room and introduced them to Alex's brother, Jerry, and Alex's assistant, Willa, who sat side by side on the single row of chairs. Hunter then joined the older man at the front of the room while the videographer recorded the scene.

The young man who'd led them to the deck came inside and told everyone to please be seated.

Renee sat between Chris and Danielle. One seat remained empty with a reserved sign on the seat. Renee remembered her own wedding ceremony in a judge's chamber. It wasn't the wedding she'd wanted, but then again, her marriage hadn't been what she'd wanted, either.

Renee turned when the door opened again. Alex stepped inside, wearing a white strapless dress, white high heels and carrying a white bag with Little Sweetie inside. Alex's smile was radiant as she walked to the empty chair and sat the bag down. She walked to Hunter and stood by his side as the justice of the peace performed the marriage ceremony.

Renee blinked back tears as the couple exchanged vows and rings. Their love for each other was clear on each of their faces.

The ceremony was over quickly and Hunter and Alex accepted their congratulations before being commandeered by the photographer, who asked everyone but the bride and groom to leave the room. The couple joined them when the motor started.

"Congratulations," Renee said as the yacht began to move out into the lake.

"Thank you," Alex said, holding Hunter's hand. "I'm glad you're all here."

"We wouldn't have missed it," Danielle said.

A waiter served them champagne. Chris raised his glass and said, "To Alex and Hunter."

Renee raised her glass to toast the couple. She sipped the champagne and was about to ask Danielle a question but stopped when she saw the longing on Tristan's face as he watched Danielle. Renee studied her glass and wondered what was going on between them.

A few minutes later, Danielle, Renee and Alex went into the room where the ceremony had been held.

"What's going on with you and Tristan?" Alex asked.

Danielle gave her a puzzled look. "There's nothing going on between us. He's my friend."

"Are you sure?" Alex asked.

"Yes. I'm sure," Danielle said.

"He doesn't look at you like a friend. He looks at you like a lover would," Renee said.

"You mean the way Chris looks at you," Danielle said and smiled.

Renee felt heat rush to her face. "Yes."

Danielle shook her head. "You've got it wrong. We're friends and business partners. That's all."

Renee shared a doubting look with Alex.

"What's going on with you and Chris?" Danielle asked.

She wasn't sure how to answer the question. "We're involved with each other."

Alex rolled her eyes. "We can see that. Are you serious about him or just fooling around?"

She was seriously in love with Chris. "We're taking it one day at a time. I really like being with him. I'm not ready to get serious again."

"I didn't think I was ready, either, but love has a way of sneaking up on you," Alex said.

Later that night as she lay in Chris's arms, Renee thought about Alex's comment. Love had certainly taken her by surprise. She only hoped that she was strong enough to survive the heartache when the love was gone.

The next day, Chris and Renee arrived at LaGuardia Airport.

Arella's workshop was located in an old, brick warehouse in a part of the city that was being reclaimed by artists of all types. There were still enough questionable people on the street to keep Chris on his guard as they exited the taxi.

Renee took his hand and they walked to the gray metal door and rang the buzzer.

"Who's there?" a woman's melodious, Caribbean voice poured from the intercom.

"Chris Foster. I spoke to you earlier." He gave Renee's hand a gentle squeeze as they were buzzed in.

They entered a brightly lit corridor. Photographs of art deco and art nouveau jewelry lined both walls.

"They're beautiful," Renee said, studying the photograph of a delicate diamond necklace.

"Thank you." An attractive woman appeared at the end of the corridor, wearing faded jeans and an old shirt. Her skin was unlined and the color of honey, her eyes the color of cognac. She had the kind of face that made it difficult to determine her age.

"Arella Laveau," he said. "This is Renee Foster. We're related to Marc Foster who was a client of yours."

"Yes. I've been trying to contact Mr. Foster for a few weeks with no success."

"He's dead," Renee said.

"Well, that would explain why I couldn't reach him. I'm sorry for your loss."

"Thank you. We're hoping you have information about a necklace," Chris said, watching the woman closely.

"You understand that I can't give you information until I have proof of who you are," she said calmly.

"I've a copy of Marc's death certificate and his

will and we both have personal identification," he said.

"Come with me, please." She led them down the corridor and into a large space. Three long work benches separated the room. Man-size windows let in light from the second floor and a complex grid of hanging lights provided additional lighting. The area had a stark feel to it. Chris noted the heavy-duty security cameras and motion detectors throughout the room. His opinion of Ms. Laveau moved up several notches, especially when she called the local FBI office to verify his identity.

"I'm sorry to keep you waiting. It appears that you are who you say you are," she said a few minutes later, returning the items to them both.

"No problem," he said, taking the papers and his ID.

"So, did Marc give you a diamond necklace?" Renee asked, her tone anxious.

"Absolutely," the woman replied.

"Do you have it? Is it here?" Renee stepped forward.

Chris put his hand on her shoulder and squeezed. He knew how anxious she was but she needed to back off.

"Of course I have it," the woman said. "I suppose you want it back."

Chris smiled and put his arms around Renee, who stared at the woman, unable to speak. "Yes. She definitely wants it back."

"Have a seat over there." She waved to one of the work benches with three stools in front of it. "I'll bring them out to you."

"Them?" Renee said as they walked to the bench.

"Yes. Mr. Foster brought several pieces of jewelry to me," she said, then walked behind a brick wall. He heard what sounded like a large metal door opening. A safe. She returned a minute later carrying a large black case. She set it on the bench and opened it.

He whistled low and long at the sight. Nestled on black cloth lay Miss Gert's diamond necklace and a pair of matching earrings. Photographs couldn't capture the sparkle and beauty of the necklace. He watched as Renee gently stroked the necklace.

He felt an overwhelming need to see her wearing the necklace. "Try them on," he said.

"Yes. Do try it on. Jewelry should be worn," Miss Laveau said, and opened a drawer and removed a large hand mirror.

Chris watched as Renee lifted the necklace with shaking hands.

She held out her hand and said, "You put it on for me, Chris."

He felt a lump in his throat. He knew how much the necklace meant to her and was humbled by her request. He took the necklace from her and placed it on her neck. Her tears of joy and the smile on her face was the most beautiful sight he'd ever seen. As he smiled, he realized that her joy was the end of his.

"Here are the pictures that Mr. Foster gave me to make the earrings." The woman removed the photos from the case.

"When did he contact you?" Renee asked.

"A few months ago. He said he tried to find me in Paris earlier, but I'd left the family business to branch out on my own. I'm glad he found me. It was a challenge and an honor to recreate a piece my grandfather designed." She smiled.

"You did an excellent job," he said.

"Thank you. I couldn't understand why Mr. Foster didn't return my calls. He'd been so insistent on me completing the design. Usually it's the client who hasn't paid who ignores my calls but he'd paid for the earrings and brought old diamond jewelry for the diamonds to use in the design."

So that's why Marc had bought so much old jewelry. He could tell by Renee's expression that she understood.

Renee picked up the earrings and put them on.

"Thank you, Miss Laveau. Aunt Gert will be absolutely thrilled. She'd sold the original pair years ago."

"Yes. He said she'd used the money to pay for her niece's extra college expenses."

He put his arms around Renee and held her as she cried.

Later, they took a taxi back to the airport to catch
their flight back to Atlanta. The jewelry had been
carefully wrapped and stored in a pouch. The pouch
was now in Renee's purse. Her purse wasn't the
best solution for transporting the jewelry, but it was
the most practical and he had a feeling that she'd
balk at having the necklace out of her sight.

Their flight had been delayed due to bad weather
and they arrived in Atlanta after midnight. They
were both too tired to drive to Birmingham.

Bringing Renee to his apartment made him nervous. When Chris opened the door and turned on
the light, he realized how barren it seemed. The lone
chair in front of the television looked stark. The
dank, closed-up smell of unlived-in space filled the
room. It was a sharp contrast to her place. Her house
was a home and his apartment was just somewhere
to occasionally sleep.

"Have a seat," he said, and closed the door behind them.

"No. I'm tired. I'd like to go to bed," she said.

He took her hand and led her to his bedroom.
Thankfully he'd washed the sheets when he left for
Birmingham almost two weeks ago. Had it just
been two weeks since he'd been with her? He
turned on the single lamp in the room.

"It's not much on decor, but I can guarantee you
the bed is comfortable."

She smiled at him. "It's fine. Is the bathroom
through there?" She nodded her head toward the door.

"Yes."

He watched as she walked across the room, then closed the door to the bathroom, and wondered how he would walk away from her. It had been so easy in the past to pack his belongings and move. He'd always been eager to go, but not this time. He feared this move would be the hardest of his life.

He stripped down to his boxers and walked to his closet to dump his clothes in the dirty clothes bag and put his pants on a hanger. He turned when he heard the door open.

She wore a pretty pink bra and matching panties; walking to the bed, she put down her purse. She brought her white dress to him and he put it on a hanger. Watching her turned him on.

He walked to the bed and sat down. "Would you show me the necklace again?"

"Sure." She reached inside her purse, removed the pouch and held it out to him.

"I want to see it on you."

She met his gaze and gave him a wicked smile, then opened the pouch. The diamonds sparkled against her skin. Donning the earrings, she slowly turned to him. Smiling, she slipped the straps of her bra off her shoulders. His mouth went dry when she unfastened her bra and slowly, slowly, pulled the lacy material down.

"Renee, you're killing me."

"Turnabout is fair play." She finally removed her bra, letting the lace garment dangle on her fingertips, then dropped it to the floor. He groaned when she wiggled out of her panties. The pleasure in her eyes was almost as erotic as her striptease. She bent her knee, her hands at her hips, back arched. "You like the necklace?" Her voice was sassy.

"I like the model wearing the necklace."

She walked to the bed, stood beside him.

He wrapped his arm around her waist and pulled her close. He laid his head on her breasts. Never had he felt such tenderness and pure lust for a woman.

"I want you, Chris." Bending down she touched her lips to his head. "I really want you out of those briefs."

He moved his hands over her hips, rubbing her buttocks, and leaned back. "If you want them off, take them off."

Smiling, her hand slid inside his briefs. Slowly, her touch moved down the length of him. He gritted his teeth as she stroked him, once, twice.

"Take them off for me," she whispered and stroked him again.

He groaned in pleasure. Moving his hands from around her, he grabbed the waistband of his briefs, lifted his hips and pulled them down.

He placed his hands on her shoulders, moving them down her breasts, her stomach, over the triangular patch of hair that covered her. "I like the way you feel," he said.

She shuddered and released her hold on him. "I like the way you feel me."

He continued to stroke her, watching as desire heightened with each movement.

A few strokes later, she moved his hand. "Condom?"

"Nightstand," he replied.

"Don't go anywhere," she whispered.

"I'm not."

She opened the drawer to the nightstand and removed a single foil.

He reached out to take it from her, but she pushed his hand away. "Allow me," she said and took her own sweet time putting it on him. "I never knew putting a condom on a man was such a turn-on," she said and moved so that her legs were on either side of his.

"Glad I could help." He rubbed the inside of her thigh, loving the feel of her soft skin.

"Chris. I'm going to take you now." She straddled his hips, her knees braced on either side of his hips.

He gripped her hips, kneading her soft flesh. Reaching down between them, she wrapped her hand around him and slowly lowered her hips.

He looked down, watching her guide him inside her warm entrance. Inch by inch, she welcomed him inside her, rocking in a lazy, rhythmic seduction. He fought the urge to thrust hard into her warm core instead; he let her set the pace. Driving him crazy with need.

A hot coil of tension swirled at the base of his

spine, growing tighter and tighter. He lost grip on his control when her inner muscles tightened around him, milking him. Her cry of pleasure and wild thrusting of her hips sent him over the edge. His deep, guttural groans filled the room as pleasure overwhelmed him.

They arrived in Birmingham the next morning shortly before ten o'clock. Renee would have gone directly to her aunt Gert's condo, but knew it would be a waste of time. Aunt Gert had plans to spend most of the day being pampered, which meant she was getting her hair, nails and makeup done before the dance.

For the first time in weeks, she could relax, but there was a feeling of restlessness inside her that she couldn't shake.

"What's wrong?" Chris asked, watching her wander around the kitchen.

He would notice. He seemed to notice everything about her. "I feel like I'm supposed to be doing something, but I don't know what." She threw up her hands in frustration.

"Everything's covered for tonight," he said.

"I know but…" She shook her head.

"You need something to do. Come on, we're leaving." He got out of the chair.

"Where are we going?"

"You'll see."

Mountain View Bowling was fairly empty. A

few teenagers gathered in a line on the other end of the building.

"I can't believe you're taking me bowling," she muttered.

"You'll like bowling." He sat in a chair and took off his street shoes.

"How do you know?" She sat down in the chair next to him and put on the rented bowling shoes. "I haven't been bowling in years."

"It involves math and you're the math queen," he said after typing in their names on the computerized score sheet.

"That's really stretching it." She laughed.

"Whatever works. You're up first."

The first gutter ball was a sign of things to come.

He didn't bother to hide his smile when she pouted. "Hold your wrist straight when you release the ball. Watch my wrist."

She watched his wrist and his butt and frowned when he made a strike. She gave him a hard look.

"What?" He held up his hands.

"How often do you go bowling?"

"I haven't been in a couple of months," he said.

She picked up her ball and concentrated on keeping her wrists straight and threw another gutter ball.

"You are the worst bowler that I've ever seen," he declared a half hour later.

"I have excellent bowling skills. I do gutter balls really well," she said.

He shook his head. "When your score is two, that's not good. Time for plan B."

She put on her shoes. "What's plan B?"

"Going to the bookstore," he said.

Ten minutes later, he followed Renee into the bookstore. He watched her scan the new-books section. The tension he'd seen on her face earlier was gone.

In the café, he tried to concentrate on the magazine he'd selected, but he kept watching Renee. The time they had together was coming to an end. He wanted to make time slow down, but it wouldn't. He would leave like he'd always done in the past. Soon, he'd be in Washington, D.C., living his life in a new city. He'd soon forget about her and the way she made him feel. Hours later, he was still trying to convince himself that he could forget her.

Arriving fifteen minutes before the dance began, they took the elevator to Aunt Gert's floor. Renee was nervous and excited. She couldn't wait to see her great-aunt's face. There was also sadness in her heart because she knew Chris would leave her soon. She wouldn't think about that now. She rang the doorbell and Aunt Gert answered.

"Don't you look lovely. Where did you find that dress?" She gave Renee a hug.

"A store in Los Angeles," Renee said. "You look great yourself."

Aunt Gert wore a silver tea-length dress and

silver shoes to match. The necklace and earrings would be the final bit of sparkle to her outfit.

"Hello, handsome." Aunt Gert greeted Chris with a smile. And handsome he was in his black suit, shirt and tie. "Hello, Miss Gert."

"Renee, bring the necklace. I want you to put it on me." She walked to the sofa.

Renee followed her. "Here, you open it." She gave her the jewelry case.

"All right. It feels like Christmas every time I open the case." She lifted the lid and screamed. "My earrings! My earrings!"

Renee laughed as her great-aunt bounced on the sofa. She laughed more when she saw the surprised looked on Chris's face.

It took ten minutes for Miss Gert to calm down. She looked like a queen wearing the jewelry. She'd nearly cried when Renee told her Marc was responsible for the earrings. Watching her reaction made him glad Marc made it possible for her to be that happy.

As he escorted them downstairs to the ballroom, he could feel his time with Renee was running out. The ballroom was decorated with a Cuban nightclub feel. The band members wore white tuxedo jackets and black pants.

Miss Gert abandoned them to dance on the dance floor in the front of the room.

They sat at one of the many tables covered with white tablecloths and candles that skirted the dance floor. "I feel like I'm on the set of *I Love Lucy,*" Renee said.

"It's not so bad, and the band is good."

Renee turned to watch the dancers. "She's happy, and that's all that matters."

Chris nodded. "She's ecstatic. I didn't think she would stop screaming."

"Jewelry like that would make any woman scream."

Chris leaned in close. "I'd rather hear that kind of scream when I make love to a woman."

She whispered in his ear, "That's a different kind of scream, baby."

He laughed. "You're right."

As the music played, he watched her and realized that he loved her. Loving her scared the hell out of him. Because loving someone meant leaving yourself open and defenseless. She would never leave Birmingham to live with him. Moving from city to city every few years. *What if he moved to Birmingham?* He didn't feel the tightening in his gut when he thought about it. He liked the city, but he had a feeling that he would like any city as long as she lived there.

He would have to be honest with her and tell her how he felt. He couldn't very well hound her about being honest if he wasn't with her.

He leaned toward her. "When can we leave?"

She smiled. "Fifteen minutes."

* * *

Gert felt like a queen as she danced with Dean. Tonight, the two people she loved the most were with her. She watched as Renee and Chris danced a few feet away.

"You look lovely tonight," Dean said.

"Thank you. You don't look bad yourself."

He smiled. "That's because I'm with you."

"I wish things were different," she said.

"I heard an interesting story on the news today. The remains of "Big Ike" Henderson were positively identified. The FBI has changed his status to deceased on their Web site."

She stopped in the middle of the dance floor and her heart began to race. "Then you can come back for good?"

"Dean Benson will be moving to Birmingham or anywhere you'd like."

She smiled, then said, "I like Birmingham."

Forty-five minutes later, Chris and Renee arrived at Renee's house. *How the hell do you tell a woman you love her?* The movies and television made it look easy. But the fact of the matter was it was damn hard. The light from the stove gave a welcoming feel to the kitchen but it didn't ease his nerves.

They'd entered the den when he decided enough was enough.

"Renee." He touched her arm.

She stopped and looked at him.

"I love you." There. He'd said it.

She looked at him with a combination of surprise and disbelief then shook her head. "No. No, you don't."

His stomach clenched. "I know how I feel. I do love you," he said softly.

She backed away from him, shaking. "No. You want me. You don't love me. I don't want you to love me."

Chris felt a part of him break into pieces. His heart ached when he saw how much she was afraid. "Hey. It's okay. It's okay," he said, reaching out to comfort her.

She backed farther away from him.

The pain of her rejection stopped him cold. He dropped his hand. "I won't touch you."

She took a deep breath and met his gaze. "I care for you, Chris, but I won't love you. I wouldn't."

He watched her walk out of the den and up the stairs, and he knew he couldn't reach her. She was too afraid, been hurt too many times. His love wasn't enough.

He walked to the couch, sat down and waited for his heart to stop breaking.

Chapter 14

The next morning

There was no reason for him to stay. Chris put the last of his things in his bag. The necklace was exactly where it should be. He'd never understand his brother's actions, but this time Marc had done something right. Miss Gert had screamed like a girl when she opened the jewelry case and saw the matching earrings nestled next to the necklace.

Mission complete. It was time for him to move on.

He looked around the bedroom for the last time. The early morning sunlight shone bright against the sheer white curtains and filled the room with light. The master bedroom had become as familiar to him as his own face. In this room, he'd found passion, comfort and love.

Last night, he'd lain awake in the extra bedroom, trying not to feel. He'd waited until he heard her go downstairs before he'd come into this room.

For the first time since he was a boy, he wanted to stay in one place. To make this house his home. But he couldn't stay another day in this house, in this room, knowing the woman he loved didn't love him. She'd been his lover and he'd been foolish to let down his guard and fall in love with her.

He loved that brainiac mind of hers. He loved her fierce loyalty to her aunt Gert and her will to put down roots. She'd made Birmingham and this house her home. He'd never had a place he'd considered home in his life, but he would stay if she asked him. She hadn't. She didn't want his love.

No. It was best that he leave while he could. He picked up his bag, took it downstairs and put it by the front door. Then he went in search of Renee to say goodbye.

She was in the kitchen. He stood inside the doorway and drank in the sight of her. The bright pink, sleeveless dress she wore showed off her feminine curves. The white apron had the phrase Kiss The Cook in bright blue letters across the front. The sight of her filled his heart with both joy and pain.

She flipped pancakes on the griddle. When she

looked up and saw him standing in the doorway, she smiled and for a moment, he thought he saw something more in her expression. Something like love. He shook his head. It was wishful thinking on his part. She'd made her feelings perfectly clear last night.

"Good morning. Have a seat. The pancakes are almost ready," she said.

His heart told him to stay, to lie to himself and pretend that he belonged here with her. He didn't belong anywhere.

"I'm not staying," he said.

Her smile faded at his words. She looked down, then carefully placed the spatula on the counter. "You're leaving." It wasn't a question, but a statement.

"Yes. You have the necklace and there's no reason for me to stay."

She turned off the stove. "I understand," she said and used the spatula to remove the pancakes.

Anger, hot and deep flowed through him. He wanted to grab the plate and smash those pancakes into the wall. His heart felt like it was being torn in half and she looked as if his leaving didn't matter to her. She wouldn't even look at him. Well, to hell with it.

"I'll send the final papers to settle Marc's estate to Terrell."

"That's fine," she said softly. "Thank you, for all your help."

He balled his hands into fists then slowly, carefully, relaxed his fingers. It was time to go before he did something crazy. "Goodbye," he said softly and walked away. He kept walking and never looked back. Afraid if he looked back, he would beg her to let him stay.

Numbing pain washed over her like an icy wind from the north. Renee stared down at the golden pancakes until she heard the front door close. It was only then that she looked up and wondered how the sun could continue to shine when her world had just fallen apart.

He'd left her and taken her heart with him. Maybe that was why she felt the ache down to the marrow of her bones. She picked up the plate full of pancakes and dropped it into the trash can. The sight of food turned her stomach.

She walked slowly, carefully, out of the kitchen and up the stairs. He'd left her like every other person she'd loved had left her. The sick fear she'd felt when he'd told her he loved her last night returned with a vengeance this morning. If this was love then she wanted no part of it.

When she reached the master bedroom, she looked at the nightstand. Gone was the book she'd given him to read, along with the mounded pile of his pocket change. He'd packed and taken everything with him.

Walking to bed, she gingerly laid on top of the

rumpled sheets, which still carried the scent of him. She reached behind her, pulling the bedspread over her. She began to shake as grief and pain washed over her like a tidal wave.

The following morning, Renee called Danielle.

"I'm sorry to bother you, I really need to talk to somebody," Renee said.

"What is it?" Danielle asked.

"I think…no, I know I'm in love with Chris."

"That's wonderful," Danielle said.

"I've messed things up with him."

"What did you do?"

Renee relayed everything that had happened between them.

"You are a really smart person, but you don't know a thing about love. You can't base your life on how your parents feel or how Marc treated us. So you have rotten parents and you had a rotten husband. That's only three people with bad karma. Other people love you, so forget them. You really need to think about your life. Imagine your life with Chris then imagine it without him. Think about what's stopping you from having the life you want."

Renee took her words to heart. She spent a long time thinking about fears and her dreams. That evening, she stood in the kitchen and admitted to herself that she was acting like a big, fat chicken. A scaredy-cat. A wuss. She'd let the man she loved walk out of her life without ever telling him that she loved him. Worse, she'd reacted as if he'd pointed a gun at her when he'd told her that he loved her, because she was afraid.

When had "I love you" come to mean "I'm leaving you" in her world? It had probably happened when she was six years old and her parents had dropped her off at boarding school. She couldn't change the past, but she could definitely change the future. She'd been so afraid of showing her feelings and having him leave her that she'd done nothing to convince him to stay. "That's just stupid," she muttered.

She wasn't stupid—far from it, but fear had clouded her vision, made her hold back, and she was darn tired of being afraid.

She wanted Chris in her life. For years, she'd hidden her true nature. He'd shown her that he loved her for herself. She had to show him that she loved him. She went to her office and began making plans. It was time, as Aunt Gert would say, to put on her big-girl panties.

The next morning, Karen Smithstone sat in the passenger seat of Renee's car. "Are you going to give me a hint?"

"You'll learn everything when we get to Aunt Gert's," Renee said, glad she'd insisted on driving. When she'd shown up at the Smithstones', Karen had fired questions like a fully automatic machine gun. "Where have you been? Why have you been avoiding me? Have you been crying? Where's Chris? Tell me. Tell me right now!"

Renee had almost changed her mind about the whole thing, but saw the concern on her friend's face and toughed it out. It hadn't taken much to get Karen to go with her to see Aunt Gert. What had been difficult was deflecting her questions. She was relieved and nervous when she parked her car in the visitors' lot.

She went to the trunk and removed two large shopping bags. "Here. Take one of these," she said, holding out one of the bags to her friend.

Karen took the bag and looked inside. "Is Miss Gert having a party and am I invited?"

For the first time in days, Renee laughed. "Sorry. No party. The rum is for her bridge club and the tequila is for her poker club and the wine is for dinner."

"She is one busy woman."

They walked into the lobby and signed in. The guard gave her a smile, but Mr. Douglass eyed the shopping bags bearing the name of a well-known wine shop.

"Ms. Foster," he said in a tone that irritated her. "Are there more than two bottles of alcohol in those bags?"

"Yes."

The man puffed out his thin chest. "Well, I'm sorry, that is against our policy. You'll have to take them back to your vehicle."

Renee shook her head. "I'm not taking them

back, Mr. Hall, and I would suggest that you review the policy. I contacted the company headquarters. They were very happy to send a copy of the new policy to my lawyer. There isn't a single thing in it that limits the amount of alcohol a resident can bring into this building."

"Young woman. I have worked here for years—"

"And—" Renee interrupted him "—you've been lying to the people who live here. I am going to go visit my great-aunt and I'm taking these—" she held up a bag "—with me."

"I will have your great-aunt thrown out of here."

Renee looked him up and down with disdain. "You don't want to mess with me and if you so much as look at Aunt Gert the wrong way, I will squash you like a bug."

He narrowed his eyes and tightened his lips, but said nothing when she and Karen headed toward the elevator.

A few residents waited at the elevators. Renee felt heat rush to her face when two older men clapped as she joined them. "That's telling that pain in the butt," one of the men said. Mr. Hall was a pain in the butt and it felt good knowing that she'd told him off and there was nothing he could do about it. Karen stared at her with a shocked look on her face.

They exited onto Aunt Gert's floor and walked the short distance down the hall to her door. Nerves she'd been battling on the drive down returned in full force when she pressed the doorbell. Aunt Gert answered the door wearing purple linen pants and a matching tunic.

"Well, come on in." She opened the door to let them enter.

Renee put the bag on the dining-room table and Karen followed suit.

"Miss Gert, Renee told the man downstairs at the sign-in desk that she was going to squash him like a bug." Karen sat down on the love seat, her eyes wide with delight.

Aunt Gert looked at Renee and raised her brow. "Is that true?"

"Yes, ma'am. He threatened to have you thrown out of here because I told him I was bringing you more than two bottles of alcohol. I had Terrell review the contract and there's no rule like that in it. If Mr. Hall gives you a hard time, you let me know."

Aunt Gert looked at her for a moment then walked to the love seat and sat next to Karen.

"I will," she said softly. "So, what is it that you want to tell us?"

Where did she begin? Then she knew exactly where to start. "I love you, Aunt Gert."

She watched as Aunt Gert's eyes filled with tears, but it was the smile on her face that let her know everything would be okay. "I know you do, sweetie," she replied, and pulled out a handkerchief from her pocket and dabbed her eyes.

Karen brushed tears from her cheeks.

"There's something you should know about Marc." Renee told them everything, beginning with the call from Chris and ending with her bringing the necklace here.

"Why didn't you tell me?" the older woman asked softly.

"I felt responsible." She held up her hand when both women protested. "I married Marc and brought him into your life and when I thought he'd stolen the necklace…" She closed her eyes, her heart pounding. "I thought you would stop loving me and treat me the way my parents treat me."

"Oh, Renee. I will never stop loving you." She left the love seat to stand in front of her, and cupped her hands around her face. "That, you can take to the bank."

Renee put her hands on top of hers and saw with clarity the love that had always been there in her aunt Gert's eyes.

Minutes and several tissues later, Aunt Gert and Karen laid down the law.

"You'd better not *ever* keep something like that to yourself again," Karen said, giving her the old hairy-eyeball look. "I love you, and friends help each other through good times and bad."

"Same goes for family," Aunt Gert added.

"Okay. I promise not to keep anything like that to myself."

"You'd better not," Aunt Gert muttered.

"Well, there is one more thing," Renee said.

"Oh, good Lord," Karen gasped. "What else?"

"I'm in love with Chris Foster." She smiled when they looked at each other and smiled back at her. "Y'all already knew."

Karen nodded. "It was pretty obvious. So when is he coming back?"

Her smile faded away. "He's not."

"What do you mean he's not?" Aunt Gert folded her arms over her chest.

"I mean he went back to Atlanta. I said some pretty bad things to him and I never told him that I love him."

Aunt Gert pursed her lips then said, "So when are you going to Atlanta to fix all this?"

Chris ignored the knock on his apartment door just as he'd ignored the calls to his cell. It was Friday night and he planned to stay inside his apartment. Alone.

He relaxed in his chair when the knocking stopped and stared at the muted television. On-screen, a car exploded, sending people on the street running for cover. He wasn't interested.

At work today, he'd learned his request for transfer to Washington, D.C., had been accepted and he should have been happy and eager to go. Instead he really didn't give a damn. There was nothing for him in D.C., just as there was nothing for him any-place if Renee wasn't with him.

Pain washed over him every time he thought of her and he couldn't stop thinking about her. With her, he didn't feel the empty restlessness, the need to always be on the lookout for the next place to go.

He swore when his cell phone rang again. He took it out of the pocket of his jeans and read the screen. It was Will.

"Hello."

"Are you home?"

He laughed. This empty apartment would never be home. "I'm at my apartment."

"Good. Now, open your damn front door."

Frowning, Chris closed his phone, walked to the door and looked out the security hole. Will stood on the other side of the door, looking impatient.

He opened the door. "What the hell are you doing here?"

"My sister's going to some charity event tomorrow. I hitched a ride with her." The ride was one of his family's private jets. Will would "hitch a ride" when the mood struck him, which was pretty often. In casual pants and a polo shirt, Will looked as if he were on his way the nearest golf course. He didn't look like he was a member of one of the wealthiest African-American families.

Will shook his head as he looked around the room. "Is there a name for the fear of furniture?"

"Shut up." Chris went to the hall closet and brought out the folding chair he'd purchased the last time Will came to his apartment. Will had made himself at home in his recliner. Chris mentally shrugged and sat in the folding chair.

"I hear your transfer request to D.C. was approved. When are you moving?"

Chris looked at him. Sometimes, like now, it still surprised him how well connected Will was with the bureau. He wondered why Will wasn't working there.

He turned and stared blindly at the television screen. "I'm not going to D.C." That surprised the hell out of him. Until he'd said the words, he hadn't realized he was thinking of not going to D.C. He'd always transferred, always moved about every two years.

For what?

The job didn't require him to move. It had always been his decision, his choice to move.

He could stay in one place if that's what he wanted. He realized that he didn't have to always be ready to leave without notice. He was moving to Birmingham…to Renee.

For the first time in days, he felt the pain fade. He'd move there and spend the rest of his life showing her, proving to her that he loved her. Smiling, Chris turned to his friend. "When do you have to leave?"

Will gave him a quizzical look. "Monday."

"Good. I need your help."

The one good thing about not having a permanent job, Renee thought as she packed the overnight bag, was the freedom to come and go as she pleased. She'd gone shopping with Karen and used the BlackBerry Alex had insisted she and Danielle use to keep in touch, to e-mail photos of the outfits she and Karen had selected for the other wives' approval.

She'd spoken with Danielle later to bring her up-to-date. Danielle had given her stamp of approval to Chris and the outfits. She told her she was sending Renee a package of scented soaps and lotions and it would arrive at her home before she left to go to Atlanta the next morning. The package had arrived a few minutes ago. When she'd opened the box she'd smiled and immediately smoothed the lotion on her hands. It smelled wonderful.

It was easy being herself around Karen, who had no trouble telling her when something was over her head, and she never made her feel uncomfortable. Except when she dragged her into an adult toy store for women. "If you're going to jump Chris, and I suggest you do, wear something that will make all the blood rush to his…"

"Karen!"

Karen rolled her eyes and began looking through the costumes. She didn't take pictures of the one she'd chosen. Chris would be the only person to *ever* see her in that getup.

Without Marc, she would never have met Alex, Danielle or Chris. For that, and Aunt Gert's earrings, she would always be grateful. She zipped the bag and carried it downstairs to the kitchen, where she'd put her purse and a map with directions to Chris's apartment. She was about to leave when her doorbell rang.

Curious, she walked to the front door and looked out one of the small, door-lite windows.

Chris stood on her porch wearing a dark gray suit, white shirt and gray striped tie. He looked cool, in control and drop-dead gorgeous. He held a large brown envelope in his hand. Her heart began to race and she opened the door.

"Hello, Renee." His voice was deep and low. The sound of it was as welcoming as a lover's touch.

"Hi." She stood motionless, just looking at the face of the man she loved. She couldn't believe he was here. She frowned. "Why are you here? Is there something wrong?"

"Nothing's wrong," he replied. "Can I come in?"

"Oh, sure." She moved back and could have kicked herself for leaving him standing on the porch. "Do you want something to drink?" she asked as she walked down the hall to the den. This was not the way she'd planned to see him again. She'd planned to shower and change at Alex's place before heading to his apartment. She had on the wrong underwear for this.

"No. I'm good."

She sat on the sofa where he'd made her scream with pleasure.

Okay, she was going to have to change her plans.

It would be here that she'd make a stand and bear her true feelings.

"What brings you here?" she asked.

"I got a renewal notice from the airport where Marc leased a hangar. In addition to leasing a hangar, Marc also rented a locker. When I went to clear out his locker, I found a key to an apartment."

"Marc had an apartment?"

"Yes. He had a room dedicated to you, Danielle and Alex."

"What do you mean dedicated?" Renee asked, interrupting him.

"I mean he kept important information on each of you. In your room, he had pictures of you and your family, a bottle of perfume you wear and even some of your clothes."

Renee didn't know what to think of this new information.

"I discovered something else in his apartment. There's no easy way for me to tell you this."

Renee braced herself. "Just tell me."

"There was a fourth room in the apartment. I believe Marc was involved with another woman."

She put her hand to her head and rubbed her temple. She was glad she was sitting because she would have fallen on her rear after hearing this. She waited, expecting to feel anger or indignation. Instead she felt sad…for Chris. And she realized that Marc's actions didn't have the power to hurt or anger her any longer. She was totally free.

"Did you contact the other woman?" she asked.

"There wasn't enough information for me to find out who she is or if Marc even married her."

"Have you told everyone?" This was the last thing Danielle and Alex needed to hear.

"No. I'll call Tristan and Hunter later. I wanted to tell you first. I'm sorry about this."

"Don't be sorry," she said. "I'm okay. His actions don't mean anything to me anymore."

He studied her face. "You're not upset." It was a statement not a question.

She shook her head. "No. Is this why you came back?"

"No. I need to give you this," he said, holding out the envelope, making no move to sit down.

"What is it?" she asked, taking it. There were no markings or writing on it.

"Open it," he said and walked to the fireplace.

She opened the envelope and removed a stack of papers, which were held together with a binder clip. Scanning the first page, she noted Chris's full name, date and place of birth. "What is this?" she asked again, turning the pages.

"Part of the file the bureau has on me."

She looked at him and frowned in confusion. "Why are you giving this to me?"

"Because I want you to know my background. I want you to know who I am." He rubbed the back of his neck. "Marc lied to you about so many things. I don't want there to be lies between us."

Between us?

"What are you saying?" she asked, afraid to jump to conclusions, watching as he walked across the room and sat down beside her.

"I'm saying that I love you, Renee. More than anything in this world."

She felt her heart melt at his words. He loved her. Her eyes filled with tears. She wanted to tell him how much she loved him, but the only sound she could make was a choked sob.

Gently he took her hand. "I know you don't love me, but give me a chance to show you how much I love you. I promise you'll never regret it."

Renee held on to his hand then took two deep breaths.

"Chris, I…" Her voice cracked.

"Wait." He let go of her hand and reached across to the envelope she'd placed beside her. He removed a smaller envelope from inside. "These are for you."

She wiped away her tears and opened it. Inside were two tickets from Birmingham to Cape Town, South Africa. A calm settled within her. She carefully put the tickets, his files and the envelops on the end table.

She reached over and took his hand in hers. She looked into his golden-brown eyes. "I have something to tell you, and I want you to promise not to interrupt until I'm done."

"I promise," he said without hesitation and she could see the concern on his face.

"I love you, Christopher Steven Foster and I'm sorry," she said, squeezing his hand, "but I'm going to have to jump you. Right now."

And she did.

Epilogue

"You know," Renee said as she slid her hand over his chest, pausing to rub her thumb over his nipple, and smiled when she felt his heartbeat quicken, "you messed up all my plans. I was supposed to leave today." Of course, she didn't mind because she was happy with the way things were, thank you very much.

After she'd jumped him on the couch, Chris had carried her upstairs to the master bedroom, leaving what was left of their clothing in a rumpled trail along the way. He'd somehow managed to pull up his pants and keep them on during the trip upstairs, which puzzled her because she distinctly remembered pushing them and his boxers off his hips one slow inch at a time.

"I saw the suitcase in the kitchen." He rested his hand on her bare hip. "Where were you going?"

She closed her eyes, enjoying the way his hands moved on her body. "To Atlanta to seduce you."

"Hmm. You would have missed me. I was out of town."

"What for?" She opened her eyes and leaned back to look at his face. His eyes were closed. He looked totally relaxed and content.

"I had a few loose ends to take care of here and there."

"Hmm." She put her head on his chest again and didn't push for answers. She knew there were things about his job that he couldn't tell her.

"I'm not moving to D.C."

She grew still. "You're not?"

"No. I put in for a transfer to Birmingham."

She leaned back, maneuvering until she was on her side resting her head on her hand. "You're moving here?"

"As soon as the transfer goes through," he said, turning on his side mirroring her position.

She smiled, pleased with him. "Okay, so you're transferring to D.C. two years from now?"

"Depends," he said, tracing her lips with his finger.

She shivered, then bit the pad of his finger. "On what?"

"Whether or not you'll marry me?"

She reached out and caressed his face. "Oh, yes. I'll marry you."

He sat up and reached under the pillow. "That's good. Now, I don't have to take these back."

"How did you get something under the pillow?" She sat up, holding the sheet to her chest.

"Talent."

She dropped the sheet when she saw the necklace. It was the one she'd admired in Arella's workshop. Renee didn't know she could be this happy, this much in love with a man. He put the necklace around her neck and leaned back. "It's pretty, but it needs something."

Frowning, she looked down at the diamond necklace nestled between her naked breasts. She pulled up the sheet to cover herself. "No, it doesn't. It's just fine exactly the way it is."

He tilted his head. "You sure?" He took her hand that was holding the sheet. "Let me see that again."

"Pervert," she said when he moved her hand down.

"Hmm. Something is definitely missing." He picked up her hand and slid a diamond ring on her finger. He brought her hand to his lips. "I love you."

She leaned forward and kissed his lips. "I love you, Chris. Always."

He smiled and pulled her into his arms. "Then consider Birmingham a permanent transfer."